I am Regina

I am Regina

SALLY M. KEEHN

A Yearling Book

Published by
Dell Publishing
a division of
Bantam Doubleday Dell Publishing Group, Inc.
1540 Broadway
New York, New York 10036

ACKNOWLEDGMENTS: For their help and encouragement, I would like to thank: my friends and colleagues of the Haycock Writers' Workshop; Judith Gorog; Patricia Gauch; Tracy Gates; my mother, Mary Miller; my husband, David; and *my* daughters, Alison and Molly.

ISBN: 0-440-40754-0

Reprinted by arrangement with The Putnam & Grosset Book Group, on behalf of Philomel Books

Printed in the United States of America

February 1993

10 9 8 7 6 5 4 3

OPM

I am Regina

Foreword

Although the following narrative is fictionalized, it is based on a true story. It happened to Regina Leininger and is dedicated to her memory.

The story begins in 1755 on a small farm near present-day Selinsgrove, Pennsylvania. . . .

Foreword

CHAPTER
One

The rows of corn stretch out before me like long lines of soldiers. For the past week, Mother, Barbara and I have been harvesting the ripened ears. Now there are just gleanings left to gather.

It is getting on to sunset. The October wind rustles through the dried stalks and I am afraid. Rumors say Indians have been attacking settlements to the north of us. Will they attack here?

The corn must be gathered. I move from stalk to stalk, watching the surrounding woods from the corner of my eye. Watching for movements that don't belong to trees and wild creatures. Indian movements.

"Aren't you finished yet?"

The words startle me and I jump.

It is my sister, Barbara, standing now before me. She balances a corn-filled basket on her hip.

"Don't creep up on me like that," I tell her.

She laughs. "Did you think I was an Indian?"

"It's not funny."

"You're like a rabbit, Regina, jumping at every sound."

I ignore her, break a ripened ear from its stalk and tear off the husk.

"Stop worrying about the Indians. Father says they'll never come over the Allegheny Mountains." Barbara is twelve, only thirteen months older than me. She thinks she knows everything.

"The Reverend Haines says they might. He heard rumors that the Allegheny Indians are on the warpath. That they have already attacked settlers ten miles north of here. Weren't you listening to him yesterday?"

"I was listening. But Regina, those settlers had built their cabins in Indian territory. This land belongs to us."

I search the wooded hills that rise to the north and west of our farm. Beyond them, I see the dark outline of the Alleghenies. The Albany Line, which divides our land from the Indians', runs through these mountains. Will the Indians respect this line?

Barbara tosses an ear of corn into my basket. "Remember that Sunday in July? After the French and Indians had defeated General Braddock's army at Bushy Run? The Reverend Haines said then that the French and Indians were planning to swarm down the Susquehanna River and wipe us out. They never came. I believe the good Reverend enjoys spreading rumors. It makes him feel important."

"Barbara! You musn't talk about a man of God like that."

"I'll talk about him as I please." Barbara's long skirt swishes against the corn stalks as she turns away from me. I can't bear her sassiness. Yet . . . I wish I had her confidence, her courage. Nothing seems to frighten her.

I watch Barbara disappear among the corn stalks and I follow one row over, keeping her light brown hair in sight. I feel uneasy. There is nothing here to protect my back.

Above the rustle of the corn stalks, I hear the sound of Penn's Creek, its water tumbling over stones. Tomorrow, Mother and John must cross this creek which borders our farm. Two oxen will pull the corn-filled wagon down the long path which leads through stands of tall fir trees to Gabriel's Mill. It is a good two-hour wagon ride. I wish my mother and my brother didn't have to go.

Barbara parts the corn stalks and joins me in my row. She takes an armful of corn from her basket and adds it to mine. "There. You have enough now." She balances her basket against her hip, slips through the split rail fence that protects our corn from livestock, and heads toward our cabin.

I scurry through the fence and hurry after her. The sun is setting behind the Alleghenies. Soon it will be dark.

We pass the orchard where the chickens, their feathers fluffed against the wind, roost in the apple trees. They look cold and lonely there. They should roost inside the barn where the cows and oxen sleep. I smell their strong rich scent as Barbara and I unload our corn into the wagon Father has parked beside the open door.

It is warm inside the barn and our cows make fine company, for they are motherly and kind.

An owl hoots somewhere in the distance. From the wooded hills? The mountains? Barbara laughs and races across the barnyard to our cabin. I run after her, stumble up the cabin steps and slam the door on the haunting sound.

Mother has supper waiting on the table. It is the venison stew we have been eating these past three days. I dip my biscuit in the gravy thickened with cabbage. It tastes good and warms me. I sneak a second biscuit from the bread basket. John grins at me from across the table and I grin back at him. John is sixteen, with dark, curly hair and brown eyes. Barbara says Marie LeRoy, who lives on the farm next to ours, is in love with him.

Barbara and I help Mother clear the table while Father and Christian smoke their pipes. My brother Christian is almost twenty. A man now. He would like to have a farm of his own. But Father needs Christian's strong, sturdy hands to help him till the soil and reap the harvest. Christian talks seriously with Father now about the smokehouse roof that needs repair. John sits with them, whittling on the wolf's head he is creating from a piece of oak.

I scrape the scraps off my pewter plate into Jack's clay bowl. The black and white dog paws my skirt, eager for his supper.

"Regina." Mother hands me another plate to clean.

"Must you go to the mill tomorrow?" I ask.

"The corn must be milled before the winter comes."

"I know."

Mother touches my downturned face. "With the corn meal, I can make johnnycakes for you." She smiles when I look up at her. My mother has a crooked smile that lights up the right side of her face but not the left—as if the left side held a secret she musn't tell.

"Will you buy maple sugar from the miller's wife?" I ask, guessing at that secret.

"We'll see."

I like maple sugar as much as johnnycakes. I hope "we'll see" means "yes." I scrape the plates while Mother wipes crumbs off the table into her cupped hand. She is small and quick and always moving. Unlike Father, who has a stillness inside him; who often rests his arms on the barnyard fence and watches in silence as the sun goes down. It is at times like these that my father's stillness worries me. He seems so far away.

Mother is like a sparrow, fluttering here and there, cleaning up the remnants of our meal. I wish I looked like her instead of like Father, tall and big boned. Most of all, I wish I had her hair. My mother's hair is soft and light brown, while mine is coarse and black. Barbara says my hair is like an Indian's. I hate her when she says it. Indians are heathens.

I feed Jack his supper. He wags his tail in appreciation, then gobbles down his meal. "Good boy," I say, running my hand along his silky hair. Jack makes me feel safe. He would warn us if an Indian approached.

13

Father shakes the embers from his pipe. He stands and takes out the Bible we keep in a wooden box that hangs on the cabin wall above the blanket chest. Father brought the Bible with him from Germany. He taught me to read from it.

We gather together before the fire. I rest my head on Mother's lap as Father reads aloud to us. It is the story of the Exodus when Moses led the Israelites out of Egypt. It reminds me of the story Father tells of our own exodus here from Germany. I was only two, but the story is alive in my memory, he has told it so often.

We sailed from Germany on a ship named *Patience*. Father says patience was needed to endure that long trip across the Atlantic. There were so many of us aboard, we had to be packed as tight as cucumbers in a pickle barrel. Our drinking water was black with worms. Cold biscuits were our daily fare. Either they were hard and stale or filled with red worms and spider's nests. We ate warm meals only three times a week. There was much sickness and disease. Many people died.

Mother says she wrapped me in the patchwork quilt I still keep upon the bed I share with Barbara. We call it the quilt of many colors, for Mother made it for us from scraps of cloth she'd sewed together into star designs of yellow, red, white and blue. The quilt warmed me when the cold wind blew off the ocean. Mother says she rocked me in her arms when I was frightened. She told me stories from the Bible and sang to me when fierce storms tossed the ship. Sometimes I wish I were two years old instead of ten. Then Mother could hold and rock me the way she used to.

Father closes the Bible and I have not been listening. Is it a sin to think of your own life when it is brought to light by God's Word? Tomorrow, I must read the passages to myself so that God will know I meant Him no disrespect.

Father bows his head and I bow mine. He thanks God for bringing us safely to this promised land of Pennsylvania. He asks God to watch over us.

Father walks slowly across the cabin and places the Bible inside its box. Mother says that when Father was young, she thought he was the strongest man in all of Germany. He could fell trees and split logs faster than any man she knew. But time and endless chores have aged him. He looks old and he is often sick. Yet now, as he turns back to us, he looks young. Perhaps it is the warm glow of firelight that softens the lines in his face. Perhaps it is the strength he always seems to gather from reading God's Word. Each night I pray God will keep my father strong. I would feel lost without him.

Mother leads us in the hymn singing. Her voice is strong and true.

> Alone, yet not alone am I,
> Though in this solitude so drear.
> I feel my Savior always nigh,
> He comes the weary hours to cheer,
> I am with Him and He with me,
> Even here alone I cannot be.

I love this hymn. It tells me that no matter how

alone I may feel, God is always near. My mother's arm encircles my shoulders as she sings. And it is then I know that here, within the warmth of my mother's arm, within her singing of this hymn, no harm will come. In bed, with Barbara snug against my back and a rising wind whispering through the leaves on the nearby apple trees, I fall asleep with this thought to comfort me.

CHAPTER
Two

I am like a bear. When the weather turns, I'd like to hole up in this warm cave I make from my patchwork quilt and remain in bed until the balm of spring awakens me.

It is not spring awakening me now.

"Time to get up!" My sister's cheeks are flushed with morning air. Her dark eyes shine. She is already dressed and ready for the day.

Frost laces the little window in the loft I share with her. The rising sun shines through, casting panes of pale light on the rough wood floor. It is too early to get out of bed. I hear Gert and Bessie mooing from the barn. They want to be milked. I wish the cows could milk themselves.

"Mother wants breakfast early. She and John must be leaving soon." Barbara leaves me to my slow waking.

I turn on my side and draw the quilt close around my shoulders, wanting to shut out the chilling air, the thought of Mother's leaving. I wish I could sleep all day and awaken at sunset when she returns.

I trace my finger along the knothole in the floorboard by my bed. The knothole is shaped like a queen, with a long, full dress and fancy crown. Mother says Regina means "queen." If I were really a queen, I would send my servants to the mill.

"Regina. Hurry up! We have to milk the cows!" Barbara calls from the room below.

"I'm coming."

My homespun dress and woolen shawl hang from pegs on the cabin wall only four short steps away. But it is chilly in the loft and the four steps feel like twenty.

I climb down the ladder into the cabin's main room where Father, John and Christian are already eating breakfast at the table. I wish that I could join them. Mother often says that I am too full of wishes. That my burden is to still myself and be thankful for my lot.

Barbara joins me at the cabin door. She is carrying the milk pails. I rub my hands together as we walk across the barnyard. I must milk Bessie. She won't let down her milk to cold hands.

Fritz and Brownie moo from their stall as we milk their mothers. "You'll get your share soon enough," I tell the calves who solemnly stare at us through the slats that keep them from their mothers. Bessie swings her head around, gazing at me with sad brown eyes. I rest my head against her flank, savoring the warmth.

Our breakfast is bread which we heat in toasting

irons over the fire. The bread is warm and chewy, but the crusts are hard. I feed them to Jack who lies at my feet, resting his chin on my shoes. Although he is partial to John, Jack always keeps me company when I am eating. He knows I will reward him.

John pokes his head through the cabin door. "The oxen are harnessed. We're ready." He winks at me.

Mother dons her cape. "Regina. Barbara. Mind the fire while I am gone."

I run to Mother and hug her. She smells of wood smoke and yeast. "I wish you didn't have to go."

"Why, Regina." She lifts my chin so that she can look me in the eyes. "Would you have us eat corn the way the cows do?"

"No . . . but the Indians . . ."

"What would the Indians want with one old woman?"

"You're not old! You're my mother!" I hug her hard.

Mother laughs, then wraps her arms around me. "And nothing keeps a mother from her family. I'll be back by sunset." She kisses me on the part which divides my hair. "See to the chores, and tomorrow I'll make those johnnycakes for you."

I hope she remembers to get the maple sugar, too.

Father helps Mother into the wagon. He hands John a whip to mind the oxen. "Don't spend time in idle talk, John. See to the corn."

"Yes, Father."

John whistles to Jack. The black and white dog leaps

19

into the wagon, sits himself down between John's feet, and cocks one black ear at me, as if he were saying, "Aren't you coming too?"

I wish I were.

Christian checks the oxen's harness. He adjusts a buckle with such care, as if this alone could assure the safety of their journey.

Father turns to Mother. "God be with you."

"And with you." Mother pulls her cape close around her.

"Giddap, Ben. Giddap, Red." John flicks the whip. Mother grabs the seat as the wagon lurches forward.

Christian and Barbara join Father and me. We watch the wagon slowly roll away. "The corn must be milled." Father says it to no one and yet to everyone. He closes his eyes.

My father does not give voice to fear, but I sense his concern. I slip my small hand into his large one. Father squeezes my hand and bows his head. I believe he is praying what I now pray, "Dear God, be their guide. Bring them safely home to us."

Mother has given chores to each day of the week. Monday is for baking, Tuesday is for washing and so on to Sunday which is given to the Lord. Today is Tuesday. My hands turn red from scrubbing clothes in hot, lye-soaped water.

Barbara helps me hang the wet clothes on a rope that runs between our cabin and the oak tree which grows a few yards from our door. When Father cleared the land, he let this tree remain. "The oak has weathered many storms. It has earned the right to stay here," Father told us. The oak is old. Maybe hundreds of years old. I love the sense of permanence it gives me.

"If we finish the chores by lunchtime, we can gather walnuts in the afternoon," Barbara says, hanging Christian's long trousers on the line.

"Can we visit Marie?" I ask, thinking of the walnut trees that grow along the path leading to her cabin.

Barbara grins. "That's what I've planned. But don't tell Father, unless he asks. He might disapprove. You know how he feels about 'Marie LeRoy and her fancy ways.'"

"I won't tell," I say, thinking of the necklace I made for Marie out of apple seeds. I can almost hear her delight when I give it to her. The dark seeds will look pretty against her pale and delicate skin.

It is lonely on the farm. Even the LeRoys, our closest neighbors, live a good ten-minute walk away. Both Barbara and I are hungry for companionship. We don't dally with our chores. We attack them.

At noon, Father and Christian return from gathering wood for our winter fires. They bring the cold, clean smell of pine into our cabin. Christian is a head taller than Father and his hair is light brown while my father's hair is gray. Yet they seem like brothers the way they share their chores. They both look tired and hungry as they sit down at the table. While Barbara and I fill their plates, they talk together in low voices about the bark they must gather this afternoon to make shingles for the smokehouse roof.

Father smiles up at me as I serve him his lunch of bread, cheese and apple cider. "I saw our clothes drying on the line. You and Barbara have been working hard. Your mother will be pleased."

I blush at his words. Father does not praise us often.

As Barbara and I fill our plates, I hear a soft rustle coming from outside our door. No one seems to mind it but me. It must be the chickens scratching through the fallen oak leaves. Or the wind, restless now with winter coming.

The rustling stops.

Yesterday, Barbara said that I was like a rabbit, jumping at every sound. And so I tell myself that perhaps the chickens have had their fill of bugs and mites. Perhaps the wind has died. But the sudden quiet is unnerving.

We join Father for the blessing. The table feels empty without Mother and John. I have been so caught up in chores, I haven't given much thought to them. They must be at the mill by now. I wish Jack had not gone with them. I miss his reassuring warmth against my legs, the weight of his chin resting on my shoes.

Jack would warn us if anyone approached.

Father bows his head. He begins to thank God for our meal when, as sudden as the quiet, the cabin door crashes open. Stunned, I stare at the sunlit doorway, imagining chickens exploding into flight, a gust of air.

Two dark figures are poised within it. They carry rifles. Aimed. At us.

And in that awful moment, I hear the sudden pounding of my heart, like raindrops on an empty, upturned barrel. I grab my sister's hand and squeeze it, as if Barbara's strength could still the pounding; drive away these figures casting shadows on our floor. These . . . *Indians.*

Christian pushes himself away from the table and Father grabs his arm. Father clears his throat while holding tight to Christian's tanned and muscled arm. "We ask for your blessing, Lord, in these, our times of trial," he prays, although he can see the Indians as clearly as I. "And may we be filled with the strength and beauty of your peace. Amen."

Father releases Christian and gives him a warning look. My brother's jaw is clenched. His hands have tightened into fists. But he obeys Father's unspoken words, remaining seated while the Indians approach our table, one on either side. The smell of bear grease fills the room. It must come from the Indians' scalp locks. From the red and black paint streaked across their faces.

The taller Indian grabs my father, yanks him out of his chair and onto his feet. Christian grips the edge of the table, his fingers turning white as stone. The Indian runs his hands up and down my father's homespun shirt, his pants. The Indian's hands are dark; his fingers, short, stubby and insistent. Father's hands are pale. They hang limply by his side, as if Father were saying, "We have no cause to war with you."

23

The Indian laughs. "You smart white man. You no carry weapon." He shoves Father backward. Father lurches against the table. A pewter plate crashes to the floor.

"Dirty savage!" Christian springs at the Indian. The Indian whips his rifle across my brother's face.

"No!" I scream, and Barbara rises to her feet. The second Indian, with two feathers in his scalp lock, aims his rifle at her.

"Barbara!" Father shouts.

I grab Barbara's arm. It takes all my strength to pull her down beside me. Barbara is foolish. She cannot fight these Indians. They have guns and knives. If we were to sit still and silent, maybe they would let us be.

Christian sprawls on the floor. His face is bruised and bloodied. Christian was always kind and gentle. He never hurt anyone. Tears well in my eyes as the tall Indian searches him for weapons, then drags him over to the bench across the table from Barbara and me. What do the Indians want? Why won't they go away?

The taller Indian . . . approaches . . . us. I cringe when his hand touches my hair. Sobbing, I stare at my plate. The bread my mother baked on Monday. Where is Mother? At the mill? Did the Indians attack the mill? I raise my eyes, searching for Father's reassurance. Father stares at Christian.

Christian is eyeing Father's hunting knife which hangs from a peg beside the fireplace. Oh, Christian, no, please, don't try.

24

The Indian with two feathers in his scalp lock grabs the knife. He laughs and runs his finger down the sharpened blade. He frightens me. He frightens me more than the tall one standing at my back.

Two Feathers turns to my father. "You have rum?"

"We have no rum," Father says.

"Then give tobacco."

Father nods to Christian. My brother's nose is bleeding. His mouth is fixed in a thin and angry line as he takes tobacco out of the pewter box Mother brought with her from Germany. He hands the tobacco to the Indian then stands behind my father, as if his strong sturdy body could protect my father's back. I cannot stop crying.

The taller Indian grabs the three-legged stool we keep before the fire. He sits down and lays his rifle across his lap. Two Feathers stands beside him.

I swallow my tears and watch the Indians fill their pipes and smoke. No one says a word. The silence makes my stomach ache. Bessie moos from her pen outside, as if this were just another day.

Father's hands are folded. They rest upon the wooden table as still as silence. My father's eyes are closed. I believe that he is praying. I wish I were beside him. I wish that I could hold his hand and feel the power of his prayer.

"What do you want from us?" Christian finally says.

Two Feathers lays his pipe on the table. He takes out the tomahawk he has kept strapped to his side. "We are

25

Allegheny Indians." His dark face turns ugly. "We are your enemies."

Two Feathers stands. He turns toward my father and my brother. Sunlight glancing through a windowpane catches the sharp edge of his tomahawk. My head feels dizzy with the burning light. I close my eyes. Out of darkness, I hear his words.

"You must all die."

CHAPTER
Three

Father and Christian are dead. Both the cabin Father built and the log barn he and Christian raised to house the cows and oxen are in flames. Smoke tears my eyes. Corn stalks whip against my face as Two Feathers drags me, sobbing, through the field. Ahead of me, the tall one prods Barbara with his rifle, herding her toward Penn's Creek. Our mouths are gagged. Our hands are bound behind our backs. I don't know why *we* have been saved.

Two Feathers's fingers bite into my arm, forcing me to stumble forward while I keep looking back. Two Feathers tomahawked Father. The tall one shot Christian. They left their bodies inside our home, then set our home on fire. Flames, like bloodied flags, rise from the oak tree's branches. Now our sleeping loft is burning. I don't want to believe what I am seeing. I can hardly breathe for seeing.

Two Feathers yanks me through the corn stalks, down the bank and into the creek where the wagon crossed this morning—the wagon that carried Mother and John away from me. When they return from the mill, they will find nothing of our home but ashes. Nothing of Father and Christian but ashes. I remember how carefully my brother's hands adjusted the buckle on a harness. The air smells of burning flesh and I feel faint.

Chilly water logs my shoes and the hem of my skirt, and I tell myself, Mother *will know* that Barbara and I have been captured. Even through her blinding tears, she'll sense it. She and John will gather the neighbors together—the LeRoys, the Bastians. Their feet will fly faster than eagles' wings. They will overcome the Indians. They will set us free.

Two Feathers pulls me up the stream bank and I drag my feet, wanting to leave a trail for an army to follow. Barbara turns, looking back at me and then beyond to the flames that rise above the stand of willow trees bordering the creek. For a moment, something in her eyes reminds me of Father, the way he used to look when he rested his arms on the barnyard fence and watched in silence as the sun went down. I want to slip my small hand into his large one. Bring him back to me. . . .

The aching minutes feel like hours as we are forced to climb a wooded hill. Mother and I once gathered hickory nuts along this path. Here is the twisted oak where we rested before returning home. Our baskets were full.

Mother *will* remember this path. She *will* see the marks left by my dragging feet.

The soil turns hard and rocky and Two Feathers jerks me off the path, through a laurel thicket and into a clearing covered with small ferns. Two Feathers shoves me to the ground. The tall one helps Barbara sit down, her back against a tree. He gestures as he now speaks to Two Feathers. His Indian words sound strange and frightening.

The tall one turns to us. "Galasko." He names himself, pointing to his chest with pride. He gestures at Two Feathers. "White man call him Tiger Claw."

Tiger Claw points to his face. And it is then I see, beneath the war paint, the ugly scars that run down the right side of his cheek. The mark of a cat.

"You stay with me," Galasko says. "Tiger Claw get more scalps."

My stomach heaves. I swallow the liquid that burns my throat and stare at the ground. I do not look up again until Tiger Claw is gone.

Galasko takes Father's pipe out of his belt. He fills it with tobacco and props himself against a tree. While he smokes, I inch myself through the featherlike ferns to Barbara. I curl up beside her and lean my head against her shoulder. She rests her head against mine and her soft hair brushes against my cheek. Light brown hair. Like Mother's . . . like Christian's. Christian's scalp lies beside the deerskin bag at Galasko's feet— the bag in which he put our pewter box, the necklace of blue glass beads that Mother liked to wear. I close my eyes, shutting out the awful sight of my

29

brother's bloody scalp, the bag. I listen to my sister breathe.

My head feels thick like cabbage soup. I must have been asleep for hours. How could I sleep after what has happened?

Barbara nudges me. Tiger Claw has returned, carrying a little towheaded girl. He lays her, slumped, beside me. More Indians, naked but for breechclouts and leggings, swarm into the clearing. I have never seen so many at one time. There must be over ten of them. I shrink at the sight of the tomahawks and rifles they brandish at the captives they now herd toward us: Jacob LeRoy, Marie's sixteen-year-old brother; Mary Anne Villars, the little Swiss girl who was visiting them; . . . *Marie.*

Stunned, I stare at her pale blue dress, now torn and dirty. A dark-skinned Indian leads her by a rope that is noosed around her neck. Her eyes alight on me. "Regina. Barbara," she gasps. The Indian jerks the rope, cutting off her breath.

Jacob moans. The Indian behind him jerks the rope binding Jacob's hands and he falls backward to the ground. Beside me, Barbara struggles to her feet. She stumbles toward Marie and Tiger Claw steps in her way. Defiantly, Barbara sidesteps him. Her hands are tied! She cannot help Marie!

Bark scrapes my arm as I inch myself up the tree, trying to stand, wanting to stop her. Tiger Claw is reaching for his tomahawk. Now he raises it above his head.

I scream, the gag muffling my cry as Galasko intervenes, grabbing Tiger Claw's descending arm. My legs are shaking. I sink back against the tree. Marie is sobbing and Galasko speaks harshly to Tiger Claw. He grabs Barbara and drags her to me.

Galasko towers over my sister. I cannot understand the words he says to her, but the anger in them makes me cringe. Barbara holds her head erect. She stares into Galasko's eyes, defying him.

Suddenly, Galasko laughs, as if he were pleased with her reckless courage. He shouts to the other Indians and several of them start laughing, too.

Something large crashes through the trees, startling us all. An Indian shouts! Jacques LeRoy's chestnut stallion leaps through the brush and into the clearing. A young Indian wearing Jacques's dark wool coat and deerskin leggings runs beside the stallion, holding the reins. Sweat streaks the chestnut's neck and darkens his quivering flanks.

The Indians flock around the high-strung horse, examining his teeth and legs. Marie's father, Jacques LeRoy, was proud of his stallion. He would never give him up. Not if he were alive.

I glance at Marie. Angry welts cover her throat. She is crying. How I ache for her.

Galasko raises his rifle in the air, gesturing that it is time to leave. The boy with the stallion takes the lead. Tiger Claw follows, carrying the towheaded girl. The Indians herd Barbara, Marie, Mary Anne, Jacob and me together. They prod us through the undergrowth to a steeply wooded hill. We struggle up the slope together in a breathless silence. Nothing seems to mark our passing but the dead leaves whispering beneath our feet.

The sun sets as we crest the hill. The Indians herd us onto an outcropping of granite. From here I can see over the trees and down to the valley where our farm lies. Penn's Creek circles its western border. Its waters shine in the fading light like a silver ribbon.

Once Mother braided my hair with a ribbon like that. Just for fancy. Where is Mother? Where is John? I hope that they are safe. Have they found our home in ashes? Do they search for us now?

I try to see their faces in my mind. All I can picture are the oak tree's branches, flaming against the sky. That and sunlight glancing off a tomahawk.

Father and Christian are dead. Nothing is the same. Nothing will ever be the same.

The night descends too quickly, bringing with it five more Indians. They strut around us, whooping and crying as they proudly display their spoils of battle: kettles, harnesses, blankets, Bibles . . . scalps.

"Mah!" Tiger Claw throws three fresh scalps at Barbara's feet.

I close my eyes, shutting out the vision I can too easily picture now: Mother's light brown hair; John's dark curls.

I rest my cheek against a cool, gray rock. I do not know why, but I think of the apple trees that bloomed in our orchard. I remember the way the wind scattered the pretty pink-tipped blossoms. My thoughts turn to apples, colored red, like the flesh that must outline the scalps before me.

I curl into a ball, wishing I, too, could die. Beside me, I feel Marie tremble. I wish someone would take these scalps away.

Long, silent minutes pass and I open my eyes. The young Indian wearing Jacques's wool coat approaches us. He gathers up the scalps and I find that now I cannot help but look at them. I hold my breath, for the threads of my life seem to hang from his hand: straight dark hair . . . but not curly like John's; red hair; blonde; no light brown hair . . . like Mother's. I let my breath out slowly, in relief. Then I start to shake. The red hair must be Mr. Bastian's, our neighbor. When I was small, Mr. Bastian used to carry me upon his shoulders. He called me his "Little Madonna," for, he said, my eyes were large and dark and he could see the sweetness of the world reflected there.

The young Indian leaves and I begin to cry: for Mr. Bastian and Jacques LeRoy; for Christian and Father; for Barbara and me.

Galasko unties our hands. He removes the gags from our mouths. He signs that we are not to talk. He gives us each a small handful of corn flour.

Marie and Mary Anne crawl to Jacob. He puts his arms around them, comforting them while they try to eat the dry corn flour. Barbara, resting against the rock next to mine, raises her hand to her mouth as if she were about to eat. "Fort Schamockin," she whispers to me. I wipe away my tears and nod, remembering the army fort located ten miles upriver from our farm. Troops must be quartered there now. Mother and John will tell them what has happened.

"Regina," Barbara whispers. She glances at the stallion grazing on a patch of grass just downhill from the rocks. She is telling me that she is going to escape. I know my sister's reckless courage. She believes that she can ride the stallion to the fort. Lead the soldiers back to us!

"No!" I whisper loudly. "Don't even try! The Indians will kill you!"

Barbara raises her finger to her lips. "Shhh."

Tiger Claw is approaching us. He settles on his haunches near my rock, keeping his eyes pinned on Barbara and me while his teeth tear into a strip of dried venison.

Barbara commences eating her corn, but I cannot eat. I need to talk to Barbara—talk her out of her foolish plan. Mother will alert the army.

I feed my share of corn to the towheaded girl who rests her head against my shoulder. She must be two, maybe three years old. When Tiger Claw looks away, I whisper, "What is your name?"

She stares at the ground. She must be afraid to talk. Or maybe she's never learned.

"I will give you a name," I whisper, putting my arm around her. "I will call you . . . Sarah."

There are no night fires. We huddle together in the darkness for warmth. Tiger Claw crouches nearby. He never leaves. Often, other Indians join him.

I do not like to look at them. They remind me of what has happened. The fierce expression on their faces tells me there will be no mercy. I am afraid of what tomorrow brings and what my sister might try to do.

And so, I gaze at Sarah, whose head is now pillowed on my lap. She twists her finger through her hair, over and over again, the way I did when I was small and frightened. Mother sang to me then, but now the sound of Indian talk and wind soughing through trees is our only lullaby.

CHAPTER
Four

We are walking single file through woods so deep the sun cannot reach us. Sarah is strapped to my back in a harness Tiger Claw has fashioned from my gray woolen shawl. The hard knots where the ends of the shawl are tied together dig into my shoulders and rub them raw. For the past three days, Tiger Claw has forced me to carry Sarah this way. This morning, when he lifted her onto my back, it felt as if a thousand knives were stabbing me. I screamed at the pain. Tiger Claw slapped me so hard my head spun.

Later, at a spring, Barbara laid wet leaves on my face to ease the swelling. She told me I must try to be brave. Be stoic like the Indians. Then I will be treated with respect. But I can't be brave when everything inside me hurts.

I wish I were Barbara. Galasko treats her more kindly than Tiger Claw does me. Now he allows Barbara and Marie to ride Jacques LeRoy's chestnut stallion at the head of our line. Galasko walks beside them, holding tightly to the reins. Shingask, the one Barbara says is Galasko's son, walks on the other side. He still wears Jacques's dark wool coat. Last night, Shingask offered Barbara and Marie strips of his dried venison to eat.

He and Galasko seem to like Barbara. Although they don't relax their watch for a single moment, they still treat her with respect. She is docile now and seems resigned to her captivity. I believe I've talked her out of trying to escape. For the past two days, she has said no more to me about it, and I am relieved. Wolves roam through these endless mountains. At night, their howls haunt our sleep. Windfall chokes the paths we follow. Barbara would be lost.

And yet, a part of me wishes she would escape. A part of me wishes she would ride the stallion over windfall and through these dark woods toward the rising sun. There she would find Fort Schamockin. There she would alert the army, lead them back to set me free. This yoke I wear is heavy. Its straps burn into my shoulders and my legs feel weak.

Sarah's breath warms my neck, reminding me that my burden is but a little girl. She lies so still upon my back. Sarah has not spoken since we began this journey. She just stares at everyone with large, blue, frightened eyes. When I was small like Sarah, Mother sang to me and told me stories.

I don't know what has happened to my mother.

Like giants, fir trees rise above us and the wind moans through their branches. "Once, long, long ago," I whisper, shutting out the lonely sound, "there lived a man named Noah."

Sarah's arms encircle my neck as I tell her the story of the endless rain and the waters that flooded all the earth. "Noah built an ark, a great boat, to sail upon the waters," I whisper, remembering the warmth of Mother's arms as she told me this story. "And then he gathered all the animals, two by two: mice, squirrels, cows, oxen, even creeping things like snakes. Hundreds of animals boarded Noah's ark, but it didn't sink."

As I tell the story, I find myself being caught up in Noah's journey across the windswept sea where waves were taller than the trees rising above us now. Tiger Claw, Galasko, Shingask—all the Indians seem to fade before the horrors of Noah's journey. I recall how I used to plead with Mother to end this story before it began, for I could not bear the tension. "Will the waves swallow Noah the way the whale swallowed Jonah?" I'd ask. "Will Noah drown?" "Will he ever find the land?"

Mother would always smile and say, "Regina. God was with Noah as He is with us now. He kept Noah safe. Listen to the story and you will see."

And so I put aside my fears and listened, as Sarah listens to me now, her head resting against my back. I believe she understands what I am saying. Whatever journey we may be on, whatever horrors block our way, God is with us too.

I think of Noah's animals at dusk when four new Indians painted red and black bring more captives, two by two, into the camp we've made beside a stream. Two small dark-haired boys cling together while a tall man with a red beard supports a heavy-set woman. Her skin and clothes are gray with dirt, as if she has not washed in months. Now there are ten of us held captive.

Barbara, Marie, Sarah and I, our table a slab of granite, sneak glances at the new captives while we devour small portions of dry corn flour, downing this supper the Indians have given us with handfuls of water we fetch from the nearby stream. Suddenly, Sarah slips out from beneath my arm. Cautiously, she approaches the little boys and offers them a fistful of bright red leaves. An Indian wearing a white man's linen shirt says something to Sarah and she drops her leaves. He laughs as she scurries back to me.

I comfort Sarah, offering her the last of my corn flour. But she will not eat. She gazes at the little boys with tear-filled eyes. Perhaps she once had brothers like these. I put my arm around her and I hold her close.

Now, around a smoldering fire, the four new Indians excitedly recount their battles to the others while the red-bearded man settles the heavy-set woman beside Jacob and Mary Anne, who share their supper by the stream. He says something to the Indian wearing the linen shirt, then walks over to our table.

Instantly, I like this man. His voice is warm and kind. He tells us his name is Peter Lick and that he often used to trade with Indians. He speaks and understands their tongue.

"Some of the Indians are Shawnee," he whispers, sitting on his haunches, watching the Indians riffle through a bag of white man's clothes. "Some are Delaware. They come from villages scattered throughout western Pennsylvania and the land bordering the Ohio River."

"Is that where they are taking us? To the Ohio River?" I ask, my throat tightening with fear. Mr. Bastian had once told me about the great Ohio. It sounded far away.

"Some of you will be taken there," he says gently. "Some to other villages. The Indians divide their captives up like spoils of battle. It is their way."

"Barbara and Regina are like sisters to me. We must not be separated," Marie says, her pale arms encircling our shoulders.

Across the clearing, the heavy-set woman begins to moan. Jacob and Mary Anne crouch over her, looking helpless as she clutches her knees, rocking back and forth in a pile of leaves. The Indian in the linen shirt grabs the woman by the hair. He pulls her head back and speaks harsh words into her upturned face. Peter Lick rushes over to intervene. The dusk fills with her moaning and our frantic whispers.

"We won't be separated—we can't be," I say, watching as Peter Lick talks to the Indian in the linen shirt while trying to comfort the woman.

"I won't let the Indians part us," Barbara says fiercely, echoing Marie's promise.

"But you and Marie belong to Galasko. While I . . . Sarah and I belong to Tiger Claw." I glance at Sarah who lays curled beside me. Sadly, she traces a finger through dead leaves.

"Perhaps Tiger Claw and Galasko come from the same village," Marie says.

"No, they don't. Their Indian words sound different," Barbara replies, her voice lower now.

The woman has stopped moaning. Peter Lick leads her over to the two small boys who huddle, shivering, beneath an ash tree. Galasko stands watch over them, his body alert and listening.

"There must be something we can do," Marie whispers.

"My mother will find us. She will set us free," I say, clinging to this hope above all others.

"Regina. Mother may . . . she may not be alive." Barbara's voice cracks as she says the words and tears well up in her eyes.

"She is alive!" I say loudly.

"Shhh." Barbara glances toward the stream. Tiger Claw is approaching us. He slaps a leather thong against his leg. I push myself away from the rock and curl around Sarah, as if we were about to sleep. Barbara and Marie settle in the leaves at my back.

It is getting dark. Even darker with Tiger Claw's shadow hovering over us. I hear his leather thong, slapping against a knee.

Only when the slapping becomes a distant echo does

Barbara whisper in my ear. "Don't worry, Regina. I'll think of something."

I can hear the desperation in her voice. "Shingask is kind," I whisper over my shoulder, feeling the familiar tears welling in my eyes. "He and Galasko will let me go with you."

"Tiger Claw will not." Barbara wraps her arms around me and Sarah then. It is the first time she has hugged me in a long, long time. I burrow my back into her warmth and I try to sleep.

Another day has passed. Barbara and Marie still ride the chestnut stallion at the head of our line. Nothing has changed except that the woods are thinner now. I can see the sky. I don't know how it can be so blue when my thoughts feel black, like thunder. We are deep in Indian territory. No white man can find us here.

Peter Lick says that soon the Indians will disband and go home to their villages. He says that's all they speak of. Barbara *must* have a plan. Earlier, I saw her speak to Galasko. Tears shone in her eyes. Perhaps she's talked him into taking me with them.

I am hungry and my throat is dry. Since daybreak, we have been trudging uphill behind the chestnut stallion. Carrying Sarah up this endless slope creates a thirst too great to bear. I don't know how trees can grow in this arid land.

I have had no water since last night. My mouth is as dry as the parched corn we ate for supper. The leather shoes I inherited from Barbara last year were not made for hard travel. The soles are coming off. They make a flapping sound as I shuffle through the leaves. They catch on twigs and stones, causing me to stumble.

Barbara's light brown hair, Marie's dark curls, are the beacons that I follow. They encourage me to place one foot before the other, to keep on going until nightfall when we can be together.

I would be lost without Barbara and Marie.

Elizabeth, the heavy-set woman, walks ahead of me, swaying from side to side, humming a strange, sad melody. Barbara says to stay away from her, for she is mad. Tiger Claw stalks behind us. I can smell the bear fat he uses on his hair and skin. I feel trapped.

Finally, we crest the hill and I hear the sound of running water. A stream must be nearby. Downhill, Galasko halts the chestnut stallion. Shingask helps Marie dismount.

I think of nothing but water. Fresh, cold water, laced with the taste of watercress. I rush downhill with Sarah hanging onto my neck. I rush away from Tiger Claw and toward the stream. The sole of my shoe catches on a rock and I stumble, falling to my knees. Sarah's weight crushes against me and she begins to cry.

Galasko shouts.

Startled, I look up. The chestnut stallion is charging through woods on the stream's far side! Barbara perches over his neck, her heels drumming against his flanks.

For an instant, I don't believe what I am seeing. This

43

couldn't be Barbara's plan! She *wouldn't* escape! Not now, after so long a time. We are too deep in Indian territory.

Abruptly, I recall how she held me through the night, her quiet desperation. "I'll think of something," she told me.

Now she and the stallion disappear, as if they were swallowed by the trees. Her reckless flight, her sudden absence hits me—like a hard blow to the stomach.

Barbara is *gone*.

Breathless, I try to stand. Tiger Claw grunts. He kicks me to the ground. Whimpering, I cover my head, expecting his next blow. Struggling to hang onto me, Sarah screams.

The Indians talk above me and Tiger Claw yanks me to my feet. Sarah clutches my neck, trying to regain her balance. I stumble over a rotted log as I am herded with the other captives to a clearing by the stream.

Galasko stands framed by the gold of poplar leaves. He raises his rifle in the air then disappears in the direction that Barbara rode. Six Indians follow him.

I wish courage for Barbara. I wish wings for the stallion's feet. I wish for the trees to part, making a path that will lead her through this wilderness to the soldiers who will return to rescue me.

My legs are shaking. I cannot seem to catch my breath. Marie lifts Sarah off my back, then she puts an arm around me. She always used to smell like violets.

Now she smells of fear. "Barbara will be all right," Marie whispers. "She is so brave."

The five remaining Indians keep us closely guarded as the minutes slowly pass. The silent minutes seem to stretch—to nine, to ten, to twenty, maybe more. The sun glances off the nearby stream, turning it to gold.

I am thirsty.

If only I could ignore the threat of the Indians' rifles. If only I could skirt the Indian in the linen shirt and walk the seven paces to the stream. . . .

Water could quench my burning thirst, my fear. Water could tell me, "Barbara will be all right."

The forest fills with a wild sound, as if a hundred wolves were howling.

"The Indians," Marie gasps, turning to me. "What are they doing? What have they done to Barbara?"

My hands feel as cold as ice.

Mary Anne hides her head in the folds of Marie's blue dress. Jacob crouches, watching the trees where Barbara disappeared.

"Your sister will die," a low voice whispers.

I turn. It is the madwoman, Elizabeth. One dark eye looks at me, the other drifts, now looking at the stream, now at Tiger Claw who slouches against a tree, his rifle resting on his forearm.

"They will build a bonfire and burn her." Elizabeth laughs.

"No," I whisper, shaking my head from side to side.

45

The howling changes pitch. Now it rings with triumph and beside us Tiger Claw starts yipping like a moon-crazed dog.

Marie tightens an arm around me. Only her arm keeps me from falling. Moments later, the chestnut stallion, riderless, trots into the clearing. His reins are dangling. The whites of his eyes roll.

CHAPTER
Five

All my hope of being rescued, of escaping from the Indians, dies when, minutes later, Galasko and Shingask emerge from the poplar trees holding Barbara up between them.

"Regina! No!" Peter cries as, throwing fear aside, I run to my sister. I stumble through the stream, Indians shouting angrily behind me, and reach for Barbara. Galasko holds his rifle up between us and tries to push me back. But the look in Barbara's eyes transfixes me and I cannot move. My bones seem to turn to ashes. Barbara's eyes look . . . stunned . . . like a badly injured fox, legs mauled by a trap. "What have they done to you?" I whisper.

Peter pulls me backward, out of the rushing water. He leads me to the other captives Tiger Claw and four other Indians guard beneath a grove of birch trees. The bark reminds me of dead people's skin, cold white and pale. I feel the dark barrels of Indians' guns focused on me now.

47

"You cannot help her," Peter whispers, as Galasko and Shingask drag my unresisting sister over to a dead ash tree standing in the center of the small clearing just a few steps away from me. Bark hangs in ragged sheets from its forked branches. Barbara's cheek and neck are gashed. Blood has stained the collar of her gray home-spun dress. Her eyes look dull and lifeless, as if all her courage has now died. I cannot bear to see it die....

Galasko wraps a rope around Barbara's waist while other Indians emerge from the forest, talking excitedly among themselves. He secures Barbara to the ash tree and I force myself to reach for him, touch the bared skin of his arm. "Please. Leave her alone. She has been hurt enough," I plead, searching his stony face for a sign of mercy.

Galasko shrugs me off, as if my fingers were flies. Desperate, I turn to Shingask who watches his father bind Barbara to the tree. Shingask must be about John's age, only sixteen. He is too young to hide the hurt I see in his eyes. He thinks Barbara has betrayed him.

"She will not run away again," I promise Shingask.

He looks away from me, and Barbara begins to cry.

Tiger Claw forces himself between Shingask and me. He holds his rifle up like a bar, forcing me backward into Marie. Five Indians with angry faces now corral our little group. They force us to move—three, four, five paces backward, until a large space filled with withered grass and brush separates us from Barbara. Mark and

Johann, the two small boys, are crying. They cling to Jacob and he puts his arms around them.

"She shouldn't have tried to run away," Mary Anne sobs, hiding within the circle of Marie's pale arm.

"She wasn't running away! She was riding to Fort Schamockin. She wanted to alert the soldiers and bring them back here. She risked her life to save us! We must save her now. Somehow, we must save her." I look from one face to another. No one will meet my gaze.

Peter casts a warning glance at the Indians surrounding us. "Speak softly," he says, keeping an eye on them. They are talking among themselves. "There's nothing we can do," Peter whispers. "There are too few of us. The Indians would kill us all."

"But . . . but they are going to burn my sister."

The dark-skinned Indian called Suckachgook now piles twigs and pine boughs at Barbara's feet. A rope binds my sister's waist to the dead ash tree. Her hands are free. Her fingers pluck aimlessly at the rope binding her, as if she cannot believe its presence.

Marie takes my hand and holds it tightly. Suckachgook pokes Barbara with a stick, as if she were an animal. I flinch, but Barbara doesn't. Tears are streaming down her face as she stares at the ground. I need to see her eyes. Meet her gaze. Let her know, everything will be all right. Even though I know . . . it won't.

An Indian with a gray blanket draped across his

shoulder starts to chant. *My sister is about to be burned alive.* Why would he want to sing? Now the others join in, as if this were a celebration.

Someone should stop this!

Galasko offers Barbara a large, black book. The cover is torn and smudged, but I can tell it is a Bible.

"He is preparing her to die," Elizabeth says.

Barbara looks at the Bible for a moment, then pushes it away.

"Take the Bible, Barbara," I whisper, thinking of all the times we read the Bible together as a family. Its words always gave us strength and the courage to go on. Barbara must not refuse them now.

Galasko grabs Barbara by the hair and pulls her head back. "You read."

"I can't read it." Barbara sobs. "This Bible. It is French. I . . . I read only German."

Galasko searches through the pile of loot the Indians took from our families. He finds another Bible. A German one.

Barbara wipes her face on her sleeve. Her long white fingers tremble, fluttering like moth's wings through the pages of the book. Now they stop, hovering over an open page. Still sobbing, Barbara begins to read aloud, "The Lord is my shepherd, I . . . I shall not want."

It is the Twenty-third Psalm, Father's favorite. He often read it to us, especially when we were sad and troubled. I can almost hear him now.

"Thou . . . preparest a table before me . . . in the

presence of mine enemies . . ." Barbara sobs so hard she cannot speak.

"Thou anointest my head with oil," I say out loud. All around me the Indians chant. "My cup overflows. Surely goodness and mercy shall follow me all the days of my life; and I shall dwell in the house of the Lord forever."

Barbara closes the Bible as I finish the psalm for her. Shingask approaches her. He is not chanting like the others. He speaks to Barbara and she listens. She shakes her head. "No run," she says.

Galasko pulls his son away.

Shingask's hands gesture as he talks to his father.

I turn to Peter Lick. "What is he saying?"

Peter strokes his red beard, listening intently. "Shingask says he does not want the brown-haired girl to burn. That she has promised him she will not run away again. That he dreamt of her . . . he dreamt that the brown-haired girl had become his wife." Peter squeezes my arm gently. He knows what these words mean to me. I feel as if I am going to be sick.

Galasko, laughing, pounds Shingask on the back.

The other Indians are chanting louder now. Suckachgook waves a torch at my sister's face then lights the brush piled at her feet. The fire begins to smolder. I can almost feel the heat. Barbara screams. Oh Lord, there must be *something* I can do.

Galasko grabs Barbara's chin. He forces her to look at him. "Shingask say he no want you die."

Tears stream down my sister's face.

"Shingask say you no run away."

"No . . ." she gasps. "No run."

Galasko looks at Shingask then at Barbara. "You be brave, like *nianque,* the wild cat. Then I know you make good Indian. You stop cry, then my son, he let you live." Galasko releases Barbara's arm. He folds his arms and watches her, the way a cat would a chipmunk. But she does not stop crying.

Smoke rises from the kindling piled at her feet. Moments later, a small, hungry flame starts licking at the twigs. A small branch next to Barbara's left foot catches fire.

If tears could quench this fire, my sister's would. I want to grab her and shake her. I want to slap her face as Mother once did mine. I shout, "Barbara! Stop crying. If you stop, the Indians will let you live!"

Small flames now leap and catch onto another, larger branch, only a foot away from the torn hem of Barbara's homespun dress. Barbara struggles against the rope that binds her to the ash tree and cries as if she will never stop.

Shingask talks to Galasko. He seems to be pleading with him. The other Indians chant. A branch near Barbara's right foot catches fire. Soon flames will engulf her.

It is then, in desperation, that I do the only thing that I can do. I sing for my sister. Although my throat is tight with fear, I sing out loud, willing my voice to drown out the awful chanting, the fire:

> *A mighty fortress is our God,*
> *A bulwark never failing;*

One by one the other captives, who stood so helplessly before, join me in singing the battle hymn by Martin Luther. Do our words touch Barbara as they touch me? Our voices fill the clearing:

> *Our helper He amid the flood*
> *Of mortal ills prevailing.*

The Indians surround us with their rifles. They aim them at us but we sing on:

> *For still our ancient foe*
> *Doth seek to work us woe*
> *His craft and power are great,*
> *And, armed with cruel hate,*
> *On earth is not his equal.*

Suckachgook bends over the fire and picks up a burning branch. He threatens little Johann with it. The boy screams as he backs away. His shirt catches fire! Peter throws him to the ground, rolling him over and over until the flames are smothered. No one is singing now.

The wide-winged shadow of a chicken hawk circles the clearing. Its darkness touches Barbara whose head is bowed.

Has something died?

Moments pass. Long moments filled with the hiss and crackle of a mounting fire. Barbara shudders. The flames are strong enough that if the wind were to gust, her skirt would catch fire. She takes a deep breath and lifts her head. Relief floods me when I meet my sister's gaze. Her dark eyes are alive with feeling. "Untie me." Her voice is full of tears, but she does not cry.

Galasko gestures to Shingask. He unties my sister's bonds and, clutching the Bible to her chest, she runs to me. She falls to her knees and I kneel beside her, so full of relief I cannot speak. Shingask stands over us, but we do not look at him. Together, Barbara and I, with nothing now but the Bible and the powerful memory of a song to sustain us, watch the dead ash tree catch fire, watch the flames lick upward to a darkening sky.

CHAPTER
Six

A sparrow perches in the tree which shadows the ground where I lie. She fluffs her feathers against the cold north wind.

I wish I were that sparrow. I have no feathers to warm me. The dress Mother made for me, from linen and wool that she wove together on her loom, is in tatters from crawling through briars and windfall. Soon I will be naked.

If I were that sparrow, I would fly over these endless hills to where our farm lies. I would nest in the oak tree which shelters our cabin.

My mind plays tricks on me. I have no cabin. It is ashes now. I saw the Indians burn it down. Saw the oak tree burn. *Oh, Father, Christian.*

I do not know where I am going. It must be somewhere west of the Allegheny Mountains. The paths we follow always lead toward the setting sun. My shoes are gone. My feet are raw. They bleed.

It is morning. Tiger Claw grunts as he stretches and

stands. From this bed I've made of fallen leaves, I watch my sparrow flit away. Perhaps she will join a flock of sparrows. They will fly together, feed on seeds. They will not be lonely, for they have each other.

I have no one now save Tiger Claw and Sarah. I try to be brave for little Sarah who sleeps so soundly beside me, blanketed with my woolen shawl. For the past two days, I've told her that someday we will reach a home somewhere. A fire will warm us and kind people will clothe our bodies. They will tend to our cuts and feed us stew rich with meat and gravy. I have not told her this is but wishful thinking; that Tiger Claw has said nothing of a home or family. But we must be going somewhere. A journey cannot last forever.

Barbara and Marie are gone. Peter Lick, Elizabeth, the others are gone. They parted from us two days ago at a fork in the Indian path. Peter told me I would be going to the Ohio region. He said the land there is gentle and rolling; rich with game and broad green meadows. He told me not to be afraid. Perhaps I would be fortunate. Perhaps I would be given to an Indian family who would care for me, who would treat me as their own. It happens.

Barbara and I cried at our parting. Barbara said, "We must be brave, Regina." Those were her last words to me.

I watched Galasko and Shingask lead the horse carrying my sister and Marie away. Barbara kept looking back. Strands of brown hair fell across her face. She smoothed them back with her long pale fingers so that she could see me. I kept repeating the words to the hymn we sang when the Indians tried to burn her—"a mighty fortress is our God." But even these words, even Sarah's warmth as she clung to me, could not fill my sudden emptiness. Barbara was all that remained of my home and family.

I try to be brave now as Tiger Claw approaches me, but Father's scalp hangs from his belt, a reminder of what Tiger Claw did, what he might do to me. There is always the crack of whiplash in his voice. I cringe as he comes near.

He barks words at me. Although my body aches from sleeping on the ground, I quickly stand and back away from him—three steps, four.

Tiger Claw unwraps the shawl from a sleepy Sarah and hands it to me. Reluctantly, I don my shawl that doubles as a harness. I feel the hard knots settle into the sores which fester on my collarbone and shoulders.

Tiger Claw lifts Sarah up from the leafy bed. She rubs her eyes, slow in awakening, then stiffens, sits like a wooden doll in Tiger Claw's arms while he carries her to me.

My shoulders burn and my back aches, for I have carried Sarah for the past six days. I say to myself, please, do not make me carry Sarah today. I will die if I must carry her.

Tiger Claw is about to place Sarah into the harness when, suddenly, I find I cannot help myself. I drop from beneath her and curl like a caterpillar.

Sarah screams on the ground beside me while Tiger

Claw beats my back and shoulders with a willow branch, over and over again. Piling pain on top of pain. I feel as if I were truly dying. Let this be the end. Dear God, I cannot go on.

But I do. As if I were outside myself, I watch Tiger Claw fit a whimpering Sarah into my harness. Sarah clutches my neck, afraid. But I find I cannot calm her anymore. I have no strength. Burden in place, I follow Tiger Claw through a darkly wooded hollow and down the narrow Indian path that seems to know no end.

These past two days, I have had nothing to eat but withered crabapples. I dream of Mother's johnnycakes as I climb through windfall. The johnnycakes are warm with venison gravy. I am sinking my teeth into one when the thorns of a locust branch pierce my feet. I scream at the pain. I scream until I am numb. I scream until I cannot think.

I am walking through the valley of the shadow of death. There is no food to eat save grubs and tree bark. There is no shelter. Blood surrounds me. It lies on the ground where my feet have trod. It stripes my back where Tiger Claw has beaten me. It fills my body but it does not keep me warm. I will never be warm again. There is frost in this wind. I feel as naked as the trees.

I ford streams. I wade through marsh and swamps. I climb mountains. I am a pack horse. Sarah rides me. Tiger Claw whips me on. Day after day after day.

CHAPTER
Seven

It must be November now. My eleventh birthday has passed and I have had no time to mark it. The cries of geese no longer fill the sky. Frost coats the ground and ice skims the wide and shallow stream we have been following southward through this wooded valley. I do not know how many days it's been since I was separated from Barbara. Maybe nine or ten.

I have seen no white people since I was parted from my sister. I have seen no towns or wagon paths. We are on the far side of the Allegheny Mountains. Giant sycamores, their trunks as thick as five large men, rise from rich bottomland. Vast herds of elk gather at the scattered salt licks. Yesterday, the south wind brought us rain. At home, the east wind brought it. This is a strange new land, a wilderness to me.

My stomach aches with hunger. Nuts and corn flour have been our only food for Tiger Claw has not stopped to hunt. But early this morning, after we had forded a rushing river and come upon this stream, Tiger Claw tied Sarah and me to a white oak tree and left us for several hours. When he returned, Tiger Claw had a deer slung over his left shoulder.

Now we grill the deer meat above a fire on a spit Tiger Claw has fashioned out of saplings. I warm my hands over the flames, impatient for the meat. Sarah plays beside me. She lines three stones up, one behind the other. She moves them, one at a time, through a maze of furrows she's created in the dirt. I know why Sarah likes this game. The stones are hers. She controls them. Sarah decides which direction each will take, what its fate will be.

Tiger Claw allows us only a small portion of cooked venison. Even though we don't have salt to season the meat, I savor the rich wild taste. Five bites and my portion is gone.

"Please, may I have more?" I ask, instantly regretting the white man's words, for Tiger Claw raises his hand, threatening me.

"No speak like white man! You are Indian now!" he says in his tongue, fixing me with dark, angry-looking eyes.

I look away, glance at the whiteness of my hands, my feet. I *am* no Indian. I *never* will be. Indians are savages! They scalp fathers, steal their children. . . .

Sarah places a small gray stone into my white palm and then another, until I hold all three. She climbs into my lap.

Sweet Sarah, trying to comfort me with gifts. I rest

my cheek against her tangled hair, wishing she could talk. I *need* her to talk to me.

Sarah feels so slight as she cuddles in my arms, no more than skin and bones. She needs food.

Tiger Claw watches us, his teeth tearing into deer meat.

Resigned, I put aside resentment, and I sign to him the way that he has taught me. "May we have more meat?"

"Too much meat make you sick," he says in his tongue. I speak and understand too many of his Indian words. I have no choice.

But Tiger Claw cannot control my thoughts. Like Sarah's stones, my white man's thoughts belong to me. She crawls out of my arms. I hand her the stones and she resumes playing with them.

Tiger Claw sits on his heels, poking the fire with a small forked branch. There is deer meat cooking on the spit, but he takes no more. Cold and hunger do not seem to bother Tiger Claw. The cat who scarred him must have given Tiger Claw unnatural power. He never seems to weaken or grow tired.

Tiger Claw lifts his eyes and they meet mine. There is an expression in them I have never seen before—a softening to their gaze. He says strange words to me. I shake my head, trying to tell him that I do not understand, hoping my ignorance will not provoke his anger.

Impatiently, he walks his fingers along the ground, meaning travel. He points to the fire, then, in quick sharp movements, outlines in the dirt the shape of houses.

He must be speaking of a *village*.

Tiger Claw makes a fist. He strikes his chest, once, at the spot where his heart beats.

Tiger Claw must be speaking of his *home*.

"Soon?" I ask him, my voice trembling.

"One night," he replies, stretching as he stands.

He cannot fathom what these words mean to me. At night, curled around Sarah with only the wind at my back, I have kept myself alive with visions of a warm cabin with a knothole in the floor. I have dreamt of a log barn filled with cattle and sweet smelling hay. I have pictured people unlike Tiger Claw—good, kind people who take Sarah and me into their arms, feed us, then wish us Godspeed as they set us free.

We douse the fire and cover its ashes with wet leaves. I slip my arms through my woolen harness, the knots settling into calloused grooves. Tiger Claw lifts Sarah to my back. I feel the hard fist of her hand clenched around her stones. I pray silently in the white man's tongue, "Lord, guide us safely to a home," while we walk the Indian path following a stream.

The next day, the sun shines weakly through a graying sky. In the afternoon, the wind picks up, bringing the scent of wood smoke. Tiger Claw halts. With his knife, he cuts down a sapling which grows along the path. In horror, I watch as he now removes my father's scalp which he's carried tucked in his belt and fixes it to one end of the sapling. He carries the gray-haired scalp dangling on the stick before him as if the scalp were a trophy.

Sarah lies uncommonly still and silent on my back. She must sense my fear. What kind of people would welcome the sight of a white man's scalp?

"We go to village," Tiger Claw says. And when I do not immediately follow him, he grips my arm, forcing me.

We pad silently down the path, just up the bank from the winding stream. "Everything will be all right," I whisper to Sarah, trying to believe my words. The land *is* gentle and rolling, unlike the Alleghenies with their steep slopes and sudden valleys. Perhaps it is speaking true. Perhaps we will be welcomed.

The smell of wood smoke grows stronger. We round a bend in the path and suddenly come upon a clearing tucked among the trees. Crude log huts with bark-shingled roofs are scattered throughout it. Animal bones litter the ground outside the huts and a deerskin, stretched out on a rack to dry, ripples in the wind.

Tiger Claw raises his left hand and halts us beneath a tall maple tree that marks the forest's edge. I search the village for orchards, neatly tended gardens. I see dry corn stalks still standing in ragged patches; charred logs jumbled in a heap within a circle of large stones. I search for a log barn and find a crudely built rectangular log house erected by the stream. This village is not what I have pictured in my dreams. This is a mistake.

Tiger Claw raises the sapling which dangles my father's scalp. He shouts a chilling cry. It sounds like a wounded rabbit, only louder.

Sarah throws her arms around my neck. Her stones tumble to the ground. Tiger Claw shouts again—a wild, savage cry that chills me to the bone, for it speaks of blood—of death.

Men, women and children pour out of the log huts. They wear torn and dirty clothes, mostly made of deerskin. Although the air is chill and damp, some children wear no clothes at all. I don't know how they can survive the cold.

Tiger Claw halloos his awful cry. The people halloo back at him. They stare at me with hate-filled eyes. If I were brave like Barbara, I would escape. Now.

"I bring you one scalp! I bring you two girls, two naked frogs, to replace our brothers who have died!" Tiger Claw yells above their cries.

The people mill around us. A small boy with a pock-marked face pinches my arm. He's hurt me! Frightened, I pull away from him. The crowd parts. An old woman, dressed in a tattered deerskin sacque, walks slowly through the path the people make for her. I touch Sarah's cheek, trying to comfort her while the woman's dark, hooded eyes appraise us. A snakeskin curls around her graying hair.

Tiger Claw speaks to her. I cannot understand all the words he says, but his tone is prideful. The old woman gives me a sharp look that speaks contempt, spits, then turns away, walking stiffly through the crowd. Now a tall, aged man with sharp, uneven teeth and wearing a necklace made of bear claws, pounds Tiger Claw on his back, as if congratulating him. He shouts to the other villagers and they disperse, talking excitedly among themselves.

I don't know what they plan to do to Sarah and me, but it cannot be good. I back away from Tiger Claw—one step, two—wanting to escape, find a hollow log, a cave to hide in. Tiger Claw's hand snakes out and grabs me. His hard fingers burn into my shoulder. I am trapped.

The Indians emerge from their huts. I shrink at the weapons they now brandish—sticks, axes, clubs. Even the children carry them. They form two lines in front of me, one line facing the other. A small boy jumps up and down, bashing his club against the ground. A dark-skinned girl shrieks, circling a sharp pointed stick through the air.

So this is our welcome. Our journey's end. We are going to be beaten by these people. Sarah starts to cry.

Tiger Claw points to a painted post which stands on the far side of the clearing, between a rack of drying meat and two upturned canoes. "You must run between my people. Run to post."

"No," I tell Tiger Claw, signing frantically that my legs are too weak to run. I point to Sarah who is still strapped to my back. Sarah will receive the burden of their blows.

"My people wait." Tiger Claw pushes me and I stumble forward into the gauntlet.

Sarah squeals as a boy whips his branch across our faces. I lift my arm, trying to protect us both and the dark-skinned girl pokes my stomach with her sharpened stick. Ahead, a lean man raises his axe, waiting to cut us down. Sarah screams. I weave to the other side and the old woman in the deerskin sacque clubs my arm and then my shoulder. Three times she clubs me. Then the old woman grabs my arm and drags me downhill, my body bruised with pain. Behind me, people shout as I stumble down a rocky bank to the stream.

Four young women join the old one at the edge of the water. I struggle to escape from them as they unstrap Sarah from my back. She kicks and screams and I throw myself at them, trying to pry Sarah out of their arms. The old woman pulls me around, grabs my dress and rips it off me.

"Sarah!" I scream as two women wade into the stream, holding Sarah up between them. They lift Sarah's thin white body up, then down into the rushing water.

Strong firm hands pull me off the bank and into the water, too. Ice flows around my hips, my waist. I am so cold I cannot scream.

A young, round-faced woman standing next to me signs for me to go under the water. To let the freezing water cover my face.

She wants to drown me.

"No!" I fight her as she tries to grab my shoulders.

"No hurt you." She pushes me down into the water. Dark, dark water covers me. I am going to die.

The next thing I know, hands are pulling upward toward the light and the round-faced woman is smiling at me. She coos as if I were a child. Cold and numb, I watch her gently wash my skin with a scrap of deerskin. For a moment, I touch her hand, grateful for this unexpected gentleness.

"No hurt you," she repeats, squeezing my arm gently.

The old woman standing on the stream bank speaks harshly to the round-faced one who washes me. Muttering angrily, the old one wades into the water. The round-faced woman backs away as the old one scrubs my skin with sand and gravel she's scooped up from the bottom of the stream. She scrubs my skin until it burns. I believe she wants to scrub it off me. I shiver, too weak now, too cold to fight.

Once we have been scrubbed, the women lead Sarah and me back up the rocky bank. At the upturned canoes, the round-faced woman speaks to the old one, then veers off from our group. She does not look back.

I don't want her to leave. Hers is the only gentleness I've known since I was separated from Barbara.

The remaining women shove Sarah and me through a torn deerskin flap into a poorly made, low-ceilinged, log hut. There are no windows to let in light, only a smoke hole in the roof. Cold drafts of air seep through cracks between the logs. Desperate for warmth, I hurry to the tiny fire burning in the center of the room. The heat it throws is sparse. Four platform beds made of saplings and covered with dark skins stand along the walls. The air is dank and smokey. This is not the home I envisioned in my dreams.

The old woman bends down and pulls out a basket from under a bed. In it are old deerskin dresses and leggings. The other women dress me in these clothes. They dress Sarah, too. The ragged clothes feel stiff and they smell of mold.

The round-faced woman stoops into the hut. Chattering happily to the others, she hands moccasins to Sarah and to me. Gratefully, I slip my bruised and frozen feet into the moccasins. They are soft and warm.

Now the four young women giggle among themselves. I stand stiffly, and, as if outside myself, watch as they paint my face with bear grease that has been dyed red. Sarah cowers as the old woman paints two red circles on her cheeks. She paints Sarah's eyelids red. Sarah looks strange. Like a white girl dressed up as an Indian. Time was when I would have laughed at her. But not now.

The expressions on the women's faces grow solemn as they lead us outside. A bonfire burns in the center of the clearing. Everyone is gathered around it. Everyone watches silently while the women bring Sarah and me before the tall, old man who wears the bear-claw necklace. A frayed, red blanket covers his shoulders. In a deep, proud voice, he begins to speak. Something important is about to happen, for beside me, Tiger Claw translates what the old man says into the white man's tongue. The words Tiger Claw has forbidden me to speak sound foreign, frightening, coming from him.

"Chief Towigh says, 'Today, your white blood has been washed away. Today, you have been adopted into a great family.'"

The old man points to me. "He says you shall be called Tskinnak, 'the blackbird,' for your hair, black as ravens' wings." He looks down at Sarah who clutches my leg, looking small and frightened. "She shall be called Quetit, 'little girl.'"

The old man pauses, staring at us with somber eyes while he places his hands upon our shoulders.

"Chief Towigh says, 'Tskinnak. Quetit. From this moment on, you will be flesh of our flesh and bone of our bone.'"

I feel the dark stares of everyone upon me. Can't they see? Beneath the paint, my skin is white. The palms of my hands, my legs, my feet are *white*.

Chief Towigh lifts his gnarled hands into the air. Tiger Claw and the other Indians around us begin to chant. Several beat on drums and shake rattles made from turtle shells.

Sarah whimpers and hides her face in my skirt as the Indians begin to dance around the bonfire. I watch the firelight flicker on their faces. Some faces are painted red and black. The Indians look like devils dancing in the firelight.

I will never be flesh of their flesh, bone of their bone. *Never.*

Now the round-faced woman pulls me into the line. Sarah cries. She holds onto my dress as the woman shows me how to do the steps. She teaches me to chant, *"Danna witchee natchepung. Danna witchee natchepung."* I do not know what the words mean, but I sing them anyway. Wanting to please the only one who's shown me any kindness. I sing the words over and over, dance with Indians and I feel as if a part of me were dying.

Sarah curls up by a brush pile and falls asleep.

My feet ache and my legs feel like heavy logs. My throat is dry by the time the dance is finally ended. The round-faced woman squeezes my hand, then leaves me standing by the fire. Sadly, I watch her walk away into the crowding darkness.

The old woman leads Sarah and me back to her hut. Inside, the fire is dying. Tiger Claw comes through the door flap. Red serpents are now painted on his black-ened cheeks.

Tiger Claw calls the old woman Mother. She calls him Son. She points to Sarah and me. "You are Indians now," she says. "You are Woelfin's daughters."

I am not the old woman's daughter. I am Regina. I will always be Regina. I live with my family on a farm near Penn's Creek.

Woelfin hugs her shoulders. "It is cold in here." She points to me. "You. Tskinnak. Gather firewood."

When I do not move, she pushes me through the door flap.

Outside, the night has fallen. I finger the dried paint on my face and shiver at the strange, shadowed land stretching out before me. Like granite rocks, dark bodies huddle around a smoldering fire and . . . there is no moon.

CHAPTER
Eight

Last night I had a dream. I was at home and my sister lay beside me in our bed. The dry scent of the straw that plumped our mattress mingled with the wet, fresh scent of the rain drumming against the roof. The muffled sound of Mother's and Father's voices came up through the worn floorboards of our loft: Father's, low and serious; Mother's, pitched a little higher, in counterpoint to his. Their comforting voices, the sound of rain and Barbara's breathing, lulled me. I snuggled beneath my quilt, feeling safe and happy.

When I reached for Barbara, I awoke to find myself holding Sarah in a hard bed made of saplings. In disbelief, I closed my eyes, wanting to return to the comfort of my dream, but the dream escaped me. I searched the gloomy hut wanting to find something to give me hope—a brightly colored quilt, a wooden table set with pewter. The old woman, Woelfin, squatted by the fire. Rancid-smelling steam rose from the brew she was stirring in an earthen pot. Tiger Claw stood over her, sharpening his hunting knife with a piece of flint.

I buried my face in my deerskin blanket and I wept. I felt so alone without my family, like a bare tree in a field of snow. Then Sarah touched my face. With her finger, Sarah traced my tears, her blue eyes asking the questions that she cannot speak. She burrowed her small body into mine and gratefully, I clung to her.

Soon after we awoke, Tiger Claw left for his hunting shelter. Woelfin said with pride that he will hunt for deer and bear meat to fill our bellies. She said that he will bring back pelts to trade for guns. Tiger Claw already has a gun. I don't know why he would need more.

Before he departed, Tiger Claw hung Father's scalp from a pole that supports this hut. I couldn't help but stare at it. The firelight gleamed off the soft gray hair, turning it to silver. Tiger Claw grunted. I glanced at him, hate burning in my heart.

Cold daylight now seeps through chinks in this log hut. I huddle by the fire and watch the flames flicker. They remind me of last night when the Indians dressed me in their clothes and painted my cheeks red. Last night I danced like an Indian. I glance upward at my father's scalp, wondering if a scalp has eyes. If Father could see me now, he would be ashamed.

My stomach aches. All I have had to eat this morning is a bowl of broth. I try to sew together the strips of deerskin Woelfin has given me. I am supposed to be making moccasins, but my hands are stiff and clumsy. Mother taught me how to sew, but not like this, with a needle made of bone and dried sinew for thread. I long for the crisp feel of linen, a fine needle to guide between the threads.

Using a bone-handled knife, Woelfin scrapes flesh from a raccoon pelt. The hut reeks with the smell of the rotten meat. Mother used to hang lavender from our kitchen rafters to sweeten the air. Woelfin should use it.

She points her knife at me. "Lazy Tskinnak. Stop poking holes in the deerskin. Go into the forest. Gather food. N'gattopui, I am hungry."

"Where is the food?" I ask, careful to speak in the Indian tongue. I sense that Woelfin, like Tiger Claw, would anger at the sound of white man's words.

Woelfin glances sideways at me. "Does the wolf ask where his prey is hiding?"

"No . . ."

"Go!"

Ice crystals blanket the north wall of the hut. I can hear the wind. I want to stay by the fire. Its flames burn bright like orange flowers. I can lose myself in them.

Woelfin's knife flashes before my face. I scurry backward and fall over Sarah who has been sleeping near the fire. I want to tell her how sorry I am, but I do not know the Indian words. I reach behind her and grab a basket from under a bed. The sound of Sarah's crying haunts me as I hurry out the door flap. I remember the morning, how Sarah's finger traced my tears.

Outside, the day is gray and chilly. A woman takes down the stretched deerskin that yesterday flapped in the wind. A dog noses the ashes of last night's fire. This village is a sad and lonely place.

I search the garden plots behind the huts for gleanings. There is nothing to be found but withered stalks and leaves. I run down the bank toward the stream. Perhaps I will find fish there. I am not sure how I will catch the fish. I have no net.

Could I catch them with my hands?

The stream is frozen. I could find a stone and crack the ice. But I don't know how to get fish out of the hole. I'll have to go back without anything to eat. Woelfin will be angry. She'll beat me.

Mother never beat me.

I rest my head against an ash tree that has rooted in the rocky bank. I watch withered leaves flutter in the wind and think of home. There I would find hams hanging in the smokehouse. I would find dried corn and wheat stored in barrels. There would be nuts and dried fruit; cheese, sweet butter, and milk standing in the spring house. Sometimes I would dip my finger into the milk and scoop out the thick white cream. I loved the rich taste of this stolen treat. And there was always fresh baked bread to eat. My mother's bread.

Thinking of her bread, I remember, how after supper

the glow of firelight touched my mother's face as she sat with her mending on her lap. Sometimes she sang. I felt so safe and loved.

If only I could hear my mother now. Her singing would reassure me, tell me, "everything will be all right."

I try to sing the hymn she often sang. My throat feels hot and tight. I can but whisper as slowly the forbidden white man's words come to me.

> *Alone, yet not alone am I,*
> *Though in this solitude so drear. . . .*

I listen to the words I sing and suddenly, as real as touch, I feel my mother's presence here—a warmth I have not felt in many days. Fingers brush across my arm. Startled, I quickly turn.

But it is not my mother. Only the round-faced woman who ducked me in the water, who gave me my moccasins and danced with me. The Indians call her Nonschetto, "the doe." I stiffen, expecting her to scold me for singing in the white man's tongue. Strangely, she does not scold. Her warm brown eyes search mine, as if she would like to know who I am. Me. Regina.

I look away, stare at the earthen pot she carries and Nonschetto lifts my chin. "Why do you cry?" she says, speaking the Indian words slowly and clearly so that I can understand.

I shake my head, afraid to answer the kindness in her voice, afraid that it might turn on me. That she will become like Tiger Claw and Woelfin and hate me.

Nonschetto clucks as if I were her chick. "Do not cry," she whispers, wiping my tears away.

I lift my empty basket. "Woelfin say find food." I stumble over the Indian words.

Nonschetto smiles. "I will show you." She picks up a stone from the rocky bank and cracks the ice. She fills her pot with water, then takes my hand and leads me up the stream bank, past a hut and down a beaten path into the forest. I marvel at how quietly she moves. Even the leaves beneath her feet are silent.

Nonschetto shows me how to strip the tender bark from the maple trees. "Bark makes good food," she says.

I nod, telling her I understand. I have never eaten maple bark. But each spring, I used to look forward to the sweet taste of the sap Father gathered from the maple trees. I chew a small piece of the bark. It is hard and bitter and I spit it out. Nonschetto laughs. "Cook bark in water, over fire. Then you eat it."

We strip the bark together in a comfortable silence, then we gather walnuts, searching under wet leaves for the blackened nuts that others have missed. I am so hungry. I crack one open and eat the meat. Nonschetto watches me, smiling her approval.

When my basket is full of bark and nuts, Nonschetto invites me into her hut. It is warm inside. A large gray dog curls by the fire. Brightly colored blankets cover the beds which line the walls. There are no torn skins or dank smell. Grass hangs from the rafters, filling the room with a dry, sweet scent. Her hut feels like home.

Nonschetto reaches into a tightly woven basket and brings out a pouch filled with corn flour. "When stomach empty, wolves bite." She makes a face. "When stomach full, they sleep." She smiles and hands the pouch to me.

Overwhelmed by her kindness, I bite back my tears and sign my thanks.

"One night, many moons ago, I leave my village, too," Nonschetto says in a soft, low voice. "My husband, Clear Sky, bring me here."

"Where is Clear Sky?" I ask, wanting to know more about Nonschetto. Does she, too, miss her home?

"Hunting," she replies.

Something whimpers behind me. I turn and see a baby strapped to a cradleboard hanging on the wall. His round face is like Nonschetto's. He looks fat and happy as he rubs his eyes, awakening.

"My son, Gokhas," Nonschetto says, her voice filled with pride.

Gokhas coos at the sound of her voice. Nonschetto takes him out of his cradleboard and suckles him. I sit by the fire and Nonschetto's dog lays her big gray head on my lap. I rub her ears and she thumps her tail against the floor. For the first time since I was captured, I feel warm and peaceful. I watch the shadows play against the tightly built log walls, drink in the scent of sweet grass and listen to Gokhas's soft suckling. I do not want to leave.

It is late when I return to Woelfin. The rank smell of

rotten meat still permeates the air. Woelfin's eyes narrow when she sees me. I quickly hand her the basket Nonschetto helped me fill with food.

I don't see Sarah anywhere. Without calling her name, I search for her. This hut is small, but the darkness can easily hide a little girl, as can the wilderness outside the village. Sarah wouldn't go out there. But maybe she would, if she were looking for me.

Panic builds inside me. I look beneath my bed. No Sarah. I look beneath Sarah's. She's not there either. Then I see Woelfin's bed. The bearskin draped across it hangs over the side, almost touching the earthen floor. I lift the bearskin.

There is Sarah! She's crouched beneath the bed in a little cave she's made. She's sucking her thumb and her face is streaked with ashes. I draw her into my arms, happy that I've found her. Sarah nestles against me and I hug her close, trying to make amends for my long absence.

"Tskinnak!" Woelfin calls me to the fire. "I show you how to make Indian bread." She mixes corn flour, walnuts and water together in a moss-green bowl that someone took great care to make, for it has been smoothly rounded and finely glazed.

I watch Woelfin pat the dough into small flat cakes and I follow her example. The dough feels stiff and grainy, unlike the soft wheat dough Mother, Barbara and I kneaded to make our bread.

We bury the cakes of dough among the hot ashes

Woelfin has made by burning strips of the dried oak bark she keeps in a basket near the fire. Sarah watches the baking bread intently as she sucks on her thumb. I can sense her hunger.

Once the bread is cooked, Woelfin dusts the ashes off a piece and holds it up in front of Sarah. *"Achpoan,"* she says.

Sarah takes her thumb from her mouth. She reaches for the bread.

Woelfin holds it out of reach "Achpoan."

"Achpoan." As easily as breathing, Sarah has said the first word I have ever heard her say.

I say, "Sarah, it is bread. It is called bread." Without thinking, I speak the words in the white man's tongue, wanting Sarah to repeat them. Bread stands for Mother, for human kindness, for Nonschetto and her baby. Bread represents a life I long to share with Sarah.

Woelfin grabs my hair. She pulls back my head. "You talk like white man, I treat you like white man. I cut you like I cut the deer." She runs her finger across my throat.

She releases my hair. Terrified, I crawl away from her. I crawl under a bed which is in a corner of the hut where spiders weave their webs. "Bread," I whisper to myself, clinging to the words. "It is called bread."

I see Woelfin's feet pad to her bed. I hear a basket scrape against the floor. Her feet pad back to me and I want to disappear. I want to be swallowed up by darkness as Jonah was by the whale.

Woelfin grabs my feet and pulls me from my hiding place. "You Indian now." She forces my mouth open and rubs a gritty powder over my tongue.

My mouth burns as if it were on fire. I pull away from Woelfin. I run from her hut. My eyes are watering. I cannot see.

I feel my way along the path that curves behind the hut. I stumble through the garden, down the stream bank. I smash a rock against the ice and drown my burning mouth in water.

When the burning stops, I stare into the water turning dark as night descends. I touch the shadowy reflection of my face—a heart-shaped face like Mother's. "I am not an Indian. I am Regina." I say the words slowly in the white man's tongue.

CHAPTER
Nine

Snow is falling. Lacy flakes drift down from the cold, gray sky. They whiten the stream bank and melt into the rushing water.

Slowly, I walk along the bank, away from the squat shape of Woelfin's hut, the garden patches where mice nestle in the straw. I carry the wooden club Woelfin gave me before she pushed me out the door flap. The club is heavy and stained with blood.

The stream winds past me like a dark linen thread. It's not frozen anymore. The warm spell we've had for the past days has thawed the ice. The stream brings me solace, for it reminds me of Penn's Creek. In summer, Barbara and I would cool our feet in its refreshing water. In winter, we'd slide along the ice in our leather shoes. I dream of stealing a canoe and paddling it down this new stream, away from Tiger Claw's village. But the forest which shadows the water is deep. Its darkness, its hidden danger, frightens me. If Barbara were beside me, perhaps I could brave the danger and escape. It pains me to think she is not here.

I stop at the willow tree whose branches arch above the water, take a sharp stone out of my deerskin pouch and carve another day's passing in the willow bark. This is the fifteenth day I have spent with Woelfin. Tiger Claw has been gone for thirteen of these days. Until he returns with the deer and bear meat that he promised, I must struggle to find food to eat.

Snowflakes land on my shoulders and my arms. I wish that they would cover me, turn me into a pile of snow. Then Woelfin could not find me and force me to do her chores.

Nothing I do pleases her. This morning I brought her firewood. "Green wood makes smoke! Green wood no good!" she screamed, kicking at the wood I'd piled neatly in a corner of the hut.

Mother would never scream if I brought her green wood. She'd be patient with my mistake and show me how to mend it.

Woelfin treats me like a servant. "Tskinnak," she growls, "fetch the water! Tan the hides! Build the fire! Hunt for food!"

Mother never made me hunt. Hunting is the worst of chores. I shiver, thinking of how Woelfin forces me to catch the vermin that burrow in the garden straw. I do not know which is worse, clubbing rats and mice or eating them.

I amble round a bend in the stream and then another, filling up the hour between late afternoon and dusk. When I return to Woelfin, I will say, "I hunted the mice for a long time. The mice are all gone."

But we will be hungry.

"Then the Lord said to Moses, 'Behold I will rain bread from heaven for you; and the people will go out and gather a day's portion every day.'" Unbidden, this Bible passage comes to me, and I take it as an omen. The Lord made good his promise to a people lost in wilderness. He will provide for me.

A low voice drifts past me now, carried by the wind. Ahead, a softly rounded shape moves lightly through the snow. It is . . . Nonschetto. I can tell by the voice, melodic and low-pitched. She sings as she gathers firewood among the trees upwind from the water. Clear Sky returned to her five days ago. For him, Nonschetto's fires burn bright. He brought her wild turkey and a deer.

Sometimes, Nonschetto shares this food with me. Clear Sky does not seem to mind. He recognizes my presence with a grunt, then goes back to whatever he is doing.

Thistle, Nonschetto's large gray dog, comes out from behind her skirt. The dog barks eagerly when she spies me and races around a brush pile, downhill to my waiting arms. She shakes herself from nose to tail, covering my dress with snow. I cannot help but giggle at Thistle's excited welcome. She treats me like a long-lost friend.

Now, solemnly, she rests her large paws on my chest and licks my face, making me feel loved.

"Thistle! Down!" Nonschetto says, approaching.

Obediently, the dog settles on her haunches, her feathery tail fanning the snow while I pat her head.

"Tskinnak. You are far from home," Nonschetto says, her kind, dark eyes searching mine.

I look back at the direction from which I've come. I cannot see the village anymore. Only tall trees and snow. I had not realized I had come this far.

"I . . . was hunting," I reply.

She notices my hands, empty save for the wooden club. "Here." She smiles and gives me half her firewood. "Tell Woelfin there are no mice in snow. Only wood."

"Thank you," I say, grateful for her thoughtfulness. I could have gathered wood myself, but it never crossed my mind. Mother used to say I was too much of a daydreamer. I believe she's right.

"Come. We will walk together." Nonschetto shifts her load of firewood, resting it on her right hip. I shift mine to my left.

Her arm warm on mine, we walk side by side, back to the village. I try to imitate the way she moves, toed-in and silent through snow-covered leaves.

Nonschetto grins at my attempt. "Soon you will walk like an Indian."

Strangely, her words do not bother me. Perhaps I wouldn't mind being at least part-Indian, if I could walk like her.

"Tskinnak," she says as we near the sweat lodge. "Tell me white man's word for the sly one with the long nose and fur like. . ." She pauses, then points toward the orange-colored sun.

"Fox," I say, surprised by her question. No one here has ever asked me about a white man's word. Woelfin beats me if I say one.

"Fox," she repeats. Nonschetto smiles at me, as if I'd given her a gift. "Tskinnak. Sometime you teach me white man's words?"

"Yes," I say. "But why?"

"I use them when we trade furs with white man. If I know words, he cannot trick me. Clear Sky will be pleased. But say nothing to him. This will be our secret." She squeezes my arm and I feel pleased, so pleased I want to teach her all the words I know. Like rabbit, bear, beaver, wolf . . .

Shrieks of happy laughter greet us as we now skirt the garden patch where yesterday I clubbed three mice. A gaggle of little children scream past, catching snowflakes in their outstretched hands.

I do not recognize Sarah at first, for she is wearing an old bearskin robe—*Woelfin's robe*. It drags along the ground behind her. I cannot imagine Woelfin lending it to Sarah. And yet . . . I can. Sarah has changed since she first spoke. Now she speaks eagerly in the Indian tongue. Hearing her speak the foreign words saddens me, but pleases Woelfin. She rewards Sarah with scraps of food

86

each time she speaks. Sarah has a sweet and winning way. Sometimes the funny things she says make Woelfin laugh.

Sarah runs up to us, her sweet face flushed with pleasure. "Quetit," she says proudly, pointing to her chest.

"Yes, you're Quetit," I reply, not bothering to correct her. I must never call her Sarah again, until we escape or an army comes.

"Nonschetto," she says, pointing to my friend.

Nonschetto pats Quetit's light blonde head. "You speak well."

"Snow!" Quetit squeals, lifting her hands into the air to catch the lacy flakes. "Woelfin!" she points to our hut. Then she pauses, scrunching up her nose, as if she smells something bad. "Tiger Claw," she whispers.

"Tiger Claw is back?" I ask.

With solemn eyes, Quetit nods her head. Then, seeing the other children streaming past our hut, she races off to join them. She is so much stronger now that she has shelter, a bed to call her own.

"Perhaps Tiger Claw has brought you deer," Nonschetto says, squeezing my arm gently.

I hope he has. Then it will not matter that I've caught no mice. But I smell no deer meat roasting over fire when I duck through our door flap. Only rum.

Tiger Claw slumps across his bed. Woelfin stands over him, talking angrily. Tiger Claw turns his eyes away from her. His bleary eyes meet mine.

"Tskinnak," Tiger Claw mumbles, patting his deerskin blanket, wanting *me* to sit beside him, as if I were an old friend . . . or a wife.

I know it is the rum that speaks and I wish he wouldn't drink it. I back away from his strange gesture and pile Nonschetto's wood in a corner of the hut.

"My son brings us no deer," Woelfin says, her voice pitched low and angry. "Only white man's corn."

"White man's corn?" I ask, thinking I have not heard her right. No one has mentioned white men living near this village.

"This corn is no good!" She shoves her earthen bowl into my hands. Her moss-green bowl is filled with hard, wrinkled kernels and crescent-shaped white worms.

"The white man builds his cabin on my hunting grounds," Tiger Claw mumbles from his bed. "The white man frightens the deer away. I take his corn and shoot him."

Woelfin glances over at the pole that holds my father's scalp. Another scalp hangs there. Brown hair.

"Did you club mice for me?" Woelfin asks, her head cocked sideways, a dark eye glittering at me.

"No," I whisper, staring at the scalp. It reminds me of clubbed mice—all brown and pink and bloody. My hands begin to tremble. I think I'm going to be sick.

"Aiii! What are we to eat?" Woelfin says.

I shake my head, trying to clear my mind of a painful memory this new scalp has evoked: the gleam of a tomahawk; death screams; two scalps—Father's and Christian's.

The earthen bowl that Woelfin gave me wobbles in my trembling hands. Suddenly, it crashes to the floor.

Stunned, I stare at the shattered pieces.

"Tskinnak is no good!" Woelfin screams, raising her hand to strike me.

I cover my ears and slowly back away from Woelfin's screams, the broken shards—one step, two, until I feel the door flap, feel cold wind chill my back. I run away from her mean hut, scrambling through the charred circle where the Indians hold their council fires. Snow, mixed with cinders, has turned wet and gray.

I remember the bleak, the frightening day my father died. His hair . . .

"No!" I scream, wanting to shut out the memory; running blindly while my head reels with the remembered crash of a cabin door slammed open; the smell of burning flesh; bloodred flames; two scalps.

Tears stream down my face as I scramble past the two upturned canoes resting against the sweat lodge, slide through mud and snow downhill to the stream.

Water rushes past my feet and I see within my mind a whole fleet of canoes. They are made of white birch bark. Indians pole them through a stream of gray and light brown hair.

There is no solace from a memory here. There is no solace anywhere. My mind burns as if it were on fire. I don't know how to make it stop.

I could drown myself in water.

A twig breaks under someone's foot. Woates, a thick-set Indian woman, approaches, walking carelessly through the sticks and dark, wet leaves strewn along the stream bank. She stares at me with curious eyes as she sways from side to side, carrying a load of firewood on her right hip.

I recall a soft low voice, an arm, footsteps strangely silent as they cross twigs and leaves.

Sobbing, I stumble around the curious Woates and up the bank. Hugging my arms, head bowed against the snow, I skirt charred logs, run toward a locust tree arching over a snug bark-roofed hut. Eyes blinded by tears, I stumble through a door flap into the only refuge that I know.

There, beside a warming fire, Nonschetto holds me in her arms. Sobbing, I try to tell her what has happened. Tell her for the first time what had gone on before. Father. Christian. Barbara. All lost. All gone. The Indian words come slowly and I cannot seem to get them right.

Nonschetto croons as she smoothes the wet hair from my face. Her dark eyes well with tears, as if she were experiencing all my pain and horror.

"My mind burns like fire," I whisper. "I want to die."

"No, Tskinnak. You will live." Nonschetto's voice is soft, but I sense the strength of iron in it. "You are a strong girl. You will weather this storm and all the storms to follow." Gently, she cups my hand in hers, places my hand on my heart so that I feel its slow and steady beating. "Tskinnak. Nonschetto will teach you."

CHAPTER
Ten

Beyond the circle of our village, up a low hill near a small clear spring, grow the sugar trees. Yesterday, Nonschetto taught me how to gather their sap. She was patient with my clumsiness, as she was the day she taught me how to make an earthen bowl. The bowl is not as fine as Woelfin's moss-green one, but she uses it.

Yesterday, along with the other women from the village, we made small incisions in the sugar trees using hatchets the Indians bought from the white man. We inserted small bark funnels into the cuts, tied wooden buckets below the funnels and waited for the chill of night to cause the golden sap to run.

Now, on this crisp morning with frost-covered leaves crackling beneath our feet, we gather the golden harvest. All of us wear deerskin leggings as well as skirts. Some wear bearskin robes; others, shawls of blanket cloth their husbands bought from traders. The tight buds on the trees tell us spring is near. But the clouds our breath makes in the air, the numbness in our fingers, tell us it's still winter.

I have lived here three moons now.

I pour the sap into the large brass kettle which hangs from a spit over the fire that Woates has kindled. She stirs the sap with a wooden paddle. "Cold nights make the sap run freely," she tells me. "Fire boils the sweet sap and makes it thick."

I dip my finger into my wooden bucket, cover my finger with golden sap and lick it clean. The sweet taste makes me hungry. This winter, Tiger Claw has caught fox and beaver and I have helped Woelfin prepare the pelts for trading. But Tiger Claw has brought us little meat.

Nonschetto knows how much I hate to club the little mice and rats. When Clear Sky brings her bear and deer meat, she shares it with Quetit, Woelfin and me. In return for her kindness, I teach her white man's words she can use in bartering with traders. Soon, she will leave me. By canoe, she and Clear Sky will travel to the river forks to trade furs for brass kettles, blanket cloth, knives and beads. I don't want her to leave.

Nonschetto pours her bucket of sap into the kettle. "Remember the sugar camp?" she asks Woates.

"Aaaii! I remember. We traveled three nights to get there. My legs ached with walking! And my arms from building shelters! This village is in a good place, for it is near the sugar trees and stream."

"Where did you live before?" I ask the women.

Nonschetto points in the direction of the rising sun. "We lived there . . . maybe three nights travel from this village. But the firewood was scarce. The ground was rocky. It soon tired of growing corn."

"I have known six villages," Woates says.

"I have known five." Nonschetto stares into the boiling sap, as if she were recalling all the places she has been.

"Will we move away from here?" I ask, the thought of leaving disturbing me. I have mapped the location of our village from scraps of knowledge the Indians have given me. It lies northeast of where the Tuscarora and Muskingum rivers meet. White men trade with Indians there. At night, I pray that these white men will discover a stream. Follow it here. Trade a kettle for one useless girl. Take me away from Tiger Claw and Woelfin.

"We will stay here many winters," Nonschetto says. "Wood is plentiful and the ground is strong."

Relieved, I stare at the sap bubbling in the kettle. Soon it will thicken and turn dark. Then we will pour it into flat wooden dishes where it will harden into sugar. I cannot think of the name the white man called the sugar tree. I used to know it.

I used to know many things. But now my memories fade like leaves plucked from a tree. At night, when I try to picture my family: the way my mother smiled, the mischievous twinkle in John's eyes when he was about to do something he shouldn't, Barbara's saucy way of tossing her hair; all I see are shadows, like those the fire casts in our hut. Frightening memories no longer burn my mind, but neither do the good ones soothe it.

Several days later, on an afternoon when Nonschetto and I are alone together, gathering firewood by the stream, I share this loss with her, for I feel as if a part of me has died.

Nonschetto picks up a branch and points to a large tree stump. Delicate green branches sprout from the trunk, defying the efforts of a woodsman to destroy the tree. "You are like this tree," Nonschetto tells me. "Your roots run deep. You may not see or remember them, but they have not died. They feed you. They give you strength to grow new life."

I stare at the stump, wondering how the tree can continue to grow. Its main trunk has been severed.

"Your new life is here, with us." Nonschetto waves her branch at the surrounding woods, the stream, the cloudless sky. "You must allow yourself to grow. Do not dwell in the sadness of the past."

"It is easy for you to say," I tell Nonschetto. "The home you came from is not so different from this one. And you are Indian while I am white."

"You speak truth. But I miss my sister, White Cloud. There are times I want to run away and be with her. She knows my heart as well as she knows her own. But then I think of Clear Sky and Gokhas and how they, too, are a part of me."

"Clear Sky and Gokhas love you. Woelfin hates me,"

I say, watching the path my moccasins make through the soggy leaves. I lift my eyes to meet Nonschetto's. "Why?"

A troubled expression crosses Nonschetto's face, as if she were about to tell me something important, something that might hurt me. "The path Woelfin travels has been choked with briars. Now she is old and bitter. You must give her time to accept you."

Nonschetto finds another piece of kindling and slowly resumes walking along the bank. I follow after her, thinking of how Woelfin's bitterness drains the blood from her lips, turns them into a thin and angry line. She seldom smiles.

Perhaps, many moons ago, someone burned her cabin, too. Killed her father and her brother. The sudden thought troubles me.

I kick a pile of wet branches aside and gather two pieces hidden in the middle of them. I test each piece to make certain it is dry. Wet kindling smolders, fills an Indian hut with smoke.

Thistle shoves her wet nose into my hand. I stroke her head as we amble through the trees. Thistle's large stomach sways from side to side. Nonschetto says that within one moon, Thistle will have puppies. I cannot wait to see them. Thistle and Nonschetto are the bright spots in my life. I feel loved when I am with them.

"Look, Tskinnak! Gokhotit is fishing!" Nonschetto says, pausing at a bend in the stream.

I peer around her. Gokhotit, Chief Towigh's son,

95

crouches on a large gray rock. Intently, he casts a grape vine into the rushing water, then flicks it out, again and again. "What does he use to attract the fish?" I ask.

"Corn," Nonschetto replies. "Perhaps you could try fishing, too. *Maschilamek,* the trout fish, is wiley, but its flesh is sweet."

"Maschilamek would be too wiley for me. I am not good at catching things. Woelfin says that I am as helpless as a wolf cub."

"Even wolf cubs grow into hunters. Look, Tskinnak. Gokhotit has caught a fish!"

The silvery, rainbowed fish flashes through the air and lands on the stream bank. My mouth waters at the thought of roasted fish. Gokhotit flashes us a smile, proud of his catch. Gokhotit must be twelve or thirteen, not much older than me. But he does not have someone like Woelfin to tell him he is helpless. That he does nothing right.

Nonschetto resumes walking and I hurry after her. Beneath our feet, scraps of birch bark litter the ground where the men have been patching their canoes for travel. Ahead of us, smoke, the color of the bark, curls upward from the village huts. Once the sight of smoke rising from a chimney was a welcoming sight to me. Now it reminds me that I must return to Tiger Claw and Woelfin.

"Tskinnak. How do you say *machque* in the white man's tongue?" Nonschetto says, pausing outside the long house the Indians call the sweat lodge. I love it

96

when she asks these questions. They make me feel important, for only I know the answers.

"Bear," I tell her.

"Boar?"

"Bear."

"I trade you one bear skin for blanket," she says proudly in the white man's tongue.

"Yes. That's good! You've been practicing the words I've taught you. I can tell. No white trader will trick you now. You understand what he is saying."

Nonschetto smoothes her long black hair away from her face. It is a gesture she uses when she is pleased. I like to please Nonschetto. She's like a mother to me.

"When the dawn breaks, I will leave with Clear Sky," Nonschetto says, reverting to the Indian tongue. "When we barter with the white man, I will use the words that you have taught me."

"I have seen Clear Sky prepare his canoe for travel. When will you return?" I say, trying to hide a loss I am already feeling.

"Within the moon," she says. "You have dug a hole the way I showed you? Lined it with leaves and stored your sugar cakes so that mice cannot eat them?"

"Yes."

"And the ground nuts. You stored them there?"

I nod.

"You will be fine. When I return, I bring meat to fill your belly."

97

"Will Thistle go with you?" I place my firewood on the ground so that I can rub the gray dog's ears.

"She will go."

I wrap my arms around Thistle's neck and she licks my face. I do not want this sweet gray dog to leave.

Tiger Claw saunters by us then, accompanied by three other braves. He kicks my pile of kindling, scattering it across the ground. "This wood is wet," he says loudly, making certain everyone can hear.

"What brains you have must be in your feet. For how then could you tell?" Nonschetto retorts, stooping to help me retrieve the wood.

The other braves laugh and enter the sweat lodge. Tiger Claw keeps silent, pretending not to hear, and saunters in behind them.

"This kindling *is* dry. I felt each piece to be certain," I say, feeling tears well in my eyes. Nothing I do pleases Tiger Claw or Woelfin. And when Nonschetto leaves, I'll have no one to turn to.

"There is nothing the matter with the wood," Nonschetto says. "Do not let Tiger Claw's words wound you. He speaks loudly to make himself feel important." She hands the kindling to me. Something about her eyes reminds me of my mother. I'm not certain what. Maybe it's the compassion I see in them.

Nonschetto signals to Thistle. The gray dog trots over to her side. "Perhaps by the time we return from trading, Thistle will have puppies for you."

"I cannot wait to see them. But . . . I wish you

didn't have to go." I hang my head, not wanting her to see my tears.

Nonschetto lifts my chin. "You are a strong girl, Tskinnak. Believe me. You will manage. Everything will be all right."

I bite my lip to keep from crying, for I remember a time, not so long ago, when my mother left me too. Nothing was all right after that.

"Come." Nonschetto takes my hand, a warm smile filling her face. "We must build our fires. The kindling you gathered is good and dry. It will burn."

CHAPTER
Eleven

Tiger Claw left the day after Nonschetto and Clear Sky paddled their canoe past me and down the stream. He handed Woelfin two pheasants and a rabbit he'd shot and said he would be traveling to the Tuscarora River. There, he would trade furs with a Frenchman named Dupré. I was relieved to see him go.

But now, the pheasant and the rabbit meat is gone. Even the bones, which I used to make a broth. Last night, when Quetit complained that she was hungry, I began reluctantly to look for Tiger Claw's return. Along with guns, he promised he would bring back blankets and food—salt, white man's bread and venison. Until he comes, we live on sugar cakes and nuts.

When I scrape away the leaves covering the hole in which I store our food, I think of Nonschetto—how she taught me how to gather sap. Little Gokhas loved the sugar cakes we made. He would kick his feet in pleasure as he sucked on one. I miss my friends. I mark the days that they've been gone in the bark of the willow tree and pray: "Lord, in the shadow of your wings, hide my friends from any danger. Bring them safely home."

Now it is late afternoon on the thirteenth day since Nonschetto and Gokhas left. Woelfin naps and the village is quiet. I play a game with Quetit and her two small friends—Stone Face, a sturdy boy with a pockmarked face, and little Nunscheach with big brown eyes and a sweet heart-shaped face. It is a game that Quetit is fond of playing.

I help the little girls build a house of twigs while Stone Face makes a confusion of interconnecting paths leading to it. The object of the game is to move the two twig dolls Quetit and Nunscheach have made through the paths until they reach the house. Inside the house sits the little corn husk doll I made for Quetit in the winter. Quetit calls her "the mother doll."

But today, Stone Face is in a contrary mood. The paths he draws with his forked stick crisscross through the spring mud outside our hut in an endless maze that Quetit and Nunscheach cannot follow. Even I cannot find the end to it.

Finally, in disgust, Quetit grabs a log and rolls it across the mud, wiping out the little paths Stone Face made and making one large one.

Stone Face scowls. He tells Quetit she has spoiled the game. He throws his stick on the ground and stalks away, his body stiff with anger. Nunscheach giggles. Tri-

101

umphantly, she and Quetit hop their dolls down the broad path and into their home.

Later, as I remove the last of the sugar cakes from the hole in which I've stored them, I think of what Quetit did. It looked so easy, taking a log, wiping out the paths someone else has made and starting anew. But it takes courage, too.

At night, while the fire smolders and Woelfin mutters angrily at the feathers she is working into an elaborate feathered cloak, Quetit climbs into my lap. "Tskinnak," she says. "I hurt." She points to her belly.

"You are hungry," I say, feeling my own belly grumble. "Here." I tighten the deerskin belt around Quetit's waist. "This will make your belly feel as if it's full. Tomorrow I will hunt for you."

"Tomorrow you hunt," she says.

"Yes," I say, dreading the thought. I wish it were summer instead of early spring. Then the forest and meadows would be full of wild food I could gather—berries, fruit and nuts.

Quetit scrambles out of my lap and over to her bed. She removes her corn husk doll from a nest of deerskin blankets. She tightens the little rope belt that holds the doll together. Then she speaks softly to the doll, repeating all the words I've said. "Tomorrow we hunt," she whispers.

Sweet Quetit. Acting like a mother to a little corn husk doll. I love her.

I reach under my bed and pull out the basket where

I've stored leftover scraps of deerskin. As I begin to sew them together into a shawl to keep Quetit warm, I hear the murmur of low voices outside our hut.

I glance at Woelfin. She stares at the door flap. The firelight flickers as it opens. Tiger Claw staggers through after twelve days' absence.

I look at him expectantly. Hoping to see a side of deer. A cake of salt. Bread.

Tiger Claw's hands look empty.

I smell rum. Again. Anger begins to build inside me. When Tiger Claw drinks, he thinks of no one but himself. We have been waiting for the food he promised. We are hungry.

"Where are the blankets that you promised us?" Woelfin says, her voice sounding cold as winter. "Where are the guns? The hunting knives? The venison?"

Tiger Claw does not answer. He stares at me. I drop my eyes and intently stitch the deerskin shawl, not wanting him to sense my anger. It might make him turn on me.

My hands move the bone needle in and out of deerskin. Tiger Claw begins speaking to his mother in a low, slurred voice. I find it hard to understand what he is saying. Something about there being no time for hunting. Something about a cache of rum.

"Drunken dog!" Woelfin screams when she discovers that his empty hands speak true, that Tiger Claw has brought us nothing but foul-smelling breath. Again.

103

"You let Dupré feed you drink! Then while you sleep, he steals our furs!"

"Dupré does not steal from me!" Tiger Claw says loudly. "At the time of roasting ears, the Frenchman will pay for the furs. I have his word!"

"Words do not warm us like the blankets we need. Words do not cut like hunting knives. You should have gone with Clear Sky. He trades with John Mountain. John Mountain is an honest man."

"John Mountain lives five nights' walk from here," Tiger Claw says. "Clear Sky has not returned. But see, I am here."

I raise my eyes as Tiger Claw staggers across the floor. "Did you see Nonschetto when you were trading?" I ask, my need to know what has happened to my friend conquering any fear I have of Tiger Claw.

"I saw no Indians but Shawnee. They carry scalping knives and guns into valleys where the white man builds his cabins. Soon the French and Indian will kill all the Yengee devils." Tiger Claw laughs, a low and ugly sound, and approaches Quetit's bed. She hastily crawls out of it and onto mine, clutching her doll.

"Where is Nonschetto?" she whispers, glancing anxiously at Tiger Claw. He slumps across her bed.

"I don't know. She should be here by now," I say.

Tiger Claw turns his back to us and he begins to snore. With a stick, Woelfin pokes at the fire, making it spit and crackle. I feel her anger and frustration. We can never depend on Tiger Claw to bring us anything but scalps and talk of war. I see dark and endless years stretch out before me, filled with constant pain and hunger.

I don't sleep well that night, for my belly aches as does my heart. I worry about Nonschetto. If war has broken out where she is trading, she might get caught in rifle fire. I worry about the safety of the white man who has built his cabins in the valleys. I worry about myself. With white man pitted against white man, no one will remember one girl captured by an Indian. I tell myself I must be strong, let my heart take courage, for the Lord upholds me even now. But my sleep is troubled. In the dark hours before dawn, it begins to rain.

Early the next morning, I awaken. The fire is burning low. I rise and feed it kindling.

Quetit joins me, rubbing her hands over the flames. "Tskinnak," she whispers, "my belly aches."

Tiger Claw snores and mumbles in his sleep. He must still be drunk. Woelfin, nestled in her bearskin robe, sleeps soundly now. But when she awakens, she will be hungry, too. My heart sinks when I think of the mice and rats I must now catch to feed us.

I pick up the club I'd left beside the door flap.

"Must we hunt mice?" Quetit asks, making a face. "I don't like them."

"We will sweeten the meat with sugar cakes," I say.

"But, Tskinnak. You said the sugar cakes were gone."

"I forgot."

"Can we hunt other things?" she asks.

As I begin to shake my head, the image of Gokhotit fishing crosses my mind. Just as quickly, I dismiss it. I don't know how to fish. I've seen no other women do it. Woelfin would mock me if I tried.

Then I think of the pit in which I've stored our sugar cakes and nuts. It's all dark and empty now.

"Even wolf cubs grow into hunters," Nonschetto once told me.

I glance at Quetit, so small and trusting. She has no one to provide her food, but me. Nonschetto is gone and Tiger Claw might as well be.

"Come," I tell Quetit with resolve, remembering how she'd made her own way to a small twig house. "Today we are going fishing. We must try to catch maschilamek, the trout, to fill your belly. You will like the flesh. Nonschetto says that it is firm and sweet."

"Maschilamek," Quetit says. She picks up the basket we use for food gathering and follows me outside. The sun is breaking through the clouds and the air smells green like fresh-cut grass.

I tie a withered bird claw to a grape vine. The knot I make looks thick and clumsy, but it should hold. I bait the claw with softened corn, then throw the line into the stream and jerk it through the water. Quetit crouches beside me, watching.

Something tugs on the vine!

I flick it the way I saw Gokhotit do. The bird claw flies out of the water.

106

The corn is not on it. Neither is maschilamek.

Quetit dances around me as I bait my hook again. "We have fed maschilamek the corn. Now he must feed us." I throw the line back in, praying that this time I will catch him.

Again maschilamek eats my corn. Again he swims away.

If I do not catch him, I will have to go back to clubbing mice. I know where they nest in the garden straw. I do not want to peel away the straw. I do not want to see the small gray bodies scurry. My flesh crawls at the thought.

I throw my line downstream and flick it though the water, making the corn look like a fast-moving yellow bug.

Maschilamek strikes.

I pull back hard and fast. My bird claw flies from the water. Maschilamek flies with it! He lands on the stream bank. I fling myself upon him. I grab his slippery body. He squirms, but I do not let him squirm away. He is big! Far bigger than the fish Gokhotit caught! And at that moment, holding the rainbowed fish within my hands, I feel a strange new sense of self-importance. No one has told me what to do or how to do it. I, Tskinnak, have done this on my own.

"Tskinnak!" Quetit cries, jumping up and down in excitement. "You have caught a fish! A big fish!" She runs ahead of me, her moccasined feet flying down the beaten path toward our hut. She stops at the door flap.

She knows not to run inside the hut. If she awakens Tiger Claw, he will be angry.

Woelfin is awake. Her eyes widen when she sees what I have caught. "Maschilamek!" she says. Her hands tremble as she takes the fish from me.

She walks stiffly to a basket and brings out a sharp-ended bone. She keeps the fish and hands the bone to me. "Cross the stream where the tree was struck by lightning. Climb the bank. You will find a clearing in the trees. Wild garlic grows there like ticks on a dog. Bring me a basketful."

"But the fish," I say, my belly rumbling with hunger.

"I will build the fire and roast the fish while you are gone. Then we will eat fresh garlic greens with it for breakfast." For one moment, a smile crosses Woelfin's face. It is the first time she has ever smiled at me.

I, Tskinnak, have made Woelfin smile!

I rush back outside. "We must gather garlic," I tell Quetit who has been waiting for me by the door flap. I feel important. Full of what I have accomplished.

Just as Quetit and I are about to enter the forest, a dog howls. Someone is entering the village. It is Clear Sky! And . . . Nonschetto is with him! She carries Gokhas on her back. Thistle follows close behind. Four little puppies crowd her flanks, awkward on their short and stubby legs. The three bigger ones are brown, like their father who belongs to Woates. The fourth one is little. He is gray-haired like Thistle.

I am so relieved and happy, I do not know what to say.

Flat Nose, Woates and the other women in the village crowd around Nonschetto. She shows them a handful of blue and red beads, a large bone-handled knife. Trading has been good. I want to join them, but I feel shy. I lead Quetit to the puppies. Thistle wags her tail and licks our faces while we pet them.

I like the little gray one best. He nuzzles my hand and tries to nurse my fingers.

I feel a warm hand on my back. "Tskinnak. You have been well?" The skin around Nonschetto's eyes crinkles as she smiles at me. I love her smile. It fills her face.

"I . . . am well."

"Tskinnak caught a fish," Quetit says. "It was big. As big as—" she stretches out her arms full length.

"That is a big fish. Tskinnak should be proud."

I cuddle the gray puppy in my arms as he happily licks my face.

"The puppies are only eight days old," Nonschetto says. "But see how strong they are? When they no longer need to nurse, I will give you one."

"Could I have this little gray one?"

"He is not as strong as the others."

"But he is strong in love. See? He kisses me."

Nonschetto laughs. She picks up the puppy and he licks her nose. "He is sweet, this one. But he is small."

109

"You once said that even little wolf cubs grow into hunters," I reply, thinking proudly of the fish I've caught.

Suddenly, behind Nonschetto, I see Woelfin approaching us. She has the old people's disease. It has stiffened her limbs and made her fingers curl like claws. I do not want to feel these fingers touching me. I grab my basket and I quickly stand.

"Nonschetto!" Woelfin says. *"N'mamentschi,* I rejoice upon your safe return!" She looks at me. "Tskinnak. Do you wait for the earth to walk? Do you think she will rise up to feed us? *Pusik!* Move!" She shoos me away.

It seems that always when I am with my friend Nonschetto, Woelfin has something for me to do.

I try not to think of her as I run off to gather garlic. I think of Nonschetto. Of how she has safely returned and of the puppy that will soon be mine. I will keep the puppy no matter what Woelfin might say. And I will feed him the fish I catch so that he will grow strong.

"Tskinnak!" Quetit catches up to me and grabs my hand. Together, we discover the clearing Woelfin spoke about. It is tucked among the trees. The clearing is small and green. Garlic grows everywhere and the sun is shining.

Quetit plays with a black beetle she has found among a pile of rocks. I crawl from one clump of garlic to the next, digging it up with the sharp-ended bone. Mud

110

cakes my hands. The air smells of rich wet earth and garlic.

"Alone, yet not alone am I." I sing the words to my mother's hymn. I sing them out loud as I gather the garlic. I think of Mother, how proud she'd be if she could see the fish I caught. I think of Nonschetto and the small gray puppy. I feel happy and . . . I feel content.

A sweet high voice starts to hum the tune I sing. I look up. It is Quetit.

Quetit is singing with me.

CHAPTER
Twelve

Tummaa. I have named the puppy Tummaa, the wolf. Nonschetto says it is a good name for him. That the puppy will grow into it and become strong like his brothers.

Woelfin scolded me when I first brought Tummaa to our hut, but he wriggled his way into her affection and she allowed him to stay. "When *Lowanachen,* the North Wind, blows and *achtu,* the deer, is scarce, you must fill our bellies before you fill his," was her one admonition.

I love to see Tummaa's small, plump body curled on the packed earth floor beside my bed when I awaken each morning. Tummaa makes this hut feel like a home. Tiger Claw ignores him, but Woelfin seems happier with Tummaa here. She often talks to him. "Tummaa," Woelfin will say, "when you are bigger, you will hunt for me, heh? Catch rabbits and squirrels?"

Tummaa will answer by rolling over on his back and wiggling happily while Woelfin strokes his belly. When I see the two of them like this, I feel myself softening, almost liking Woelfin. Tummaa has created one small, but living link between us.

Sweet Tummaa follows Quetit and me everywhere. When we go to the clearing where we first gathered garlic, Tummaa rolls happily in the grass then watches me, head on his paws, while I teach Quetit forbidden words that she must never speak when we are near Tiger Claw and Woelfin.

Ever since Quetit hummed the tune while I sang my mother's song, I have felt compelled to share these white man's words with her, for they come from God and they give courage to the small and weak.

Already, Quetit knows the Lord's prayer word for word. And she's learned many of the Bible stories. I tell Quetit, "These stories form our white man's roots. They give us strength."

"I am a strong girl," Quetit will reply, flexing her arm the way she's seen Stone Face do. Then Tummaa will climb into her lap and lick her face, making Quetit giggle.

Now Tummaa lies in the shade of a maple tree. He snaps at flies while, nearby, I hoe the corn in our garden patch. I like the way Tummaa keeps an eye on me. He makes me feel loved.

The corn is as high as my shoulders. When I planted it, I fed the seed with fish heads. Squash grows beneath each stalk. Its broad green leaves protect the roots from the glaring sun. At home, we did not plant our crops this way, but it makes sense to me.

I wish these broad, green leaves could cover and protect the white man. Last night Chief Towigh lit the council fire. He announced that the French and Indians have captured the English garrison, Fort Granville. The men spoke long into the night. Tiger Claw wanted to join the other Delaware Indians fighting the English. But Chief Towigh said his warriors should wait until fall. Then, after trading furs for ammunition, they will have the powder and lead they need to kill all the Yengee devils.

Last night as I watched the hot flames of the council fire lick the sky, I could almost feel it burning.

The ground is hard and dry. My arms grow tired of hoeing. I wish that I were small like Quetit. She and the other children play tag along the border of the garden patches. They are supposed to be chasing crows away.

I hear Gokhas's high squeal. Nonschetto's baby waddles through the deep shade of a nearby oak, his arms outstretched. Nonschetto catches him and lifts him high above her head. Gokhas giggles.

"Tummaa!" I call. The gray puppy stretches. He trots over to me, his tail wagging. We join Nonschetto and her baby.

"Hello. You have bread to eat?" Nonschetto signs with her hands in the Indian way as she speaks the white man's words that I have taught her.

I sign back, "I have no bread."

Nonschetto laughs. "You sign well." She pats the

114

ground beside her. "Come. Sit with me." She gives me a piece of bread and offers Gokhas her breast. He frets and pushes himself away from her. Nonschetto reaches into her pouch and brings out dried venison. She chews the meat, then gives the softened bits to Gokhas. Tummaa climbs into her lap, looking for handouts. She does not disappoint him.

Quetit screams as she runs over to us. Stone Face chases her with a stick. Quetit hides behind me.

"Quetit stole my lucky stone! The pink one I found by the stream!" Stone Face yells, his pocked face red with anger.

"It is my stone!" Quetit says, hiding her hands behind her back. She's grown stronger since she's learned the Indian words to claim her right.

"Mine!" Stone Face says, his short, stocky legs set defiantly on the ground.

"Give him back the stone, Quetit. I will find you another one," I say. I understand her need to possess small things, but I also know that I must teach her not to steal. Quetit regards me as she would a mother. Sometimes this makes me feel important. Sometimes, it scares me. I am only eleven winters old.

"Give Stone Face his rock," Nonschetto says, "and I will tell you a story."

"The one about Meesing?" Quetit asks eagerly.

"What do you know about Meesing?" Nonschetto asks, a smile playing at the corners of her mouth.

"He's big! And he is hairy! His face is red and black

and his eyes glow in the dark." Quetit makes a face. "And Meesing smells. Like rotten eggs."

"Yes, but what does Meesing do for us?" Nonschetto asks.

"He protects all the little animals," Quetit says. "Sometimes, if children are weak, he frightens sickness out of them. And if the children are very bad, he carries them off in a bag of snakes!"

Nonschetto laughs. "Good! You remember what I've told you! And today, I will tell you a new story. One my mother taught me."

Quetit opens her hand at these words and Stone Face grabs his pink rock. He runs away to join the other children. Quetit lies down beside Nonschetto and rests her head upon her lap, seemingly content with the fairness of the trade—a story for a stone.

Gokhas tries to push Quetit away. I take him in my arms. He giggles as I rub my face into his belly.

I love the time we spend with Nonschetto beneath the oak tree. For the past several days, she has shared her stories with us here. We can listen to them with no fear of Woelfin's scolding. In the heat of the day, Woelfin sleeps.

"Once, long ago, there was a land of happy people who lived above the sky," Nonschetto begins, smiling at Gokhas who settles contentedly in my arms. "There was no sickness or death in this land. The Chieftan of the Skies who ruled it was good and kind.

"Now in this land there was no sun, for a beautiful

tree with white blossoms provided light. The Chieftan of the Skies dreamt that if this tree were not plucked up by its roots, he would die. And so, he called on his four brothers and together they uprooted the tree. It fell with a crash and knocked a large hole in the ground.

"Imagine the Chieftan's surprise when he looked down this hole! For through it he could see a bright blue sky. He called to his wife who was with child. 'Come and see!'

"They knelt beside the hole, shoots from the fallen tree of light blooming all around them, and the Chieftan said to his wife, 'You shall create a new world in the sky that lies below us, for I have dreamt this and it must be so.' Then he pushed her down the hole.

"The frightened woman fell through endless sky. Tiny birds flying by told her, 'Do not be afraid.' They gathered into a flock beneath her and bore her safely on their wings to a great blue sea. There they set her upon a mud turtle's back.

"The woman rested while water fowl and animals dove into the water to find bits of earth. They placed the dirt they'd found on the turtle's back. Soon there was enough earth for the woman to walk on.

"The mud turtle said to the woman, 'I will stay here forever to support you and all the other generations to come.'

"The land on the turtle's back continued to grow. Soon, grass and trees covered it.

"Now the woman who fell from the sky gave birth to

a daughter. And when the daughter became a woman she walked into the sea and from this union, became pregnant with twin boys. The Good Twin was born the normal way. But the Bad Twin came out from under his mother's armpit and he killed her. The grandmother buried her daughter with her feet toward the sunrise and corn grew from her body.

"The Good Twin, Sapling, smiled on the earth. He created the sun and moon to give us light. He made plants and animals and man to hunt the deer. But the Bad Twin, Flint, scorned the Good Twin's creation. He hid the animals in caves. He created all the frightening things, like bats and snakes and thunderstorms." Nonschetto pauses. Her eyes have a faraway look, as if she were thinking about such a storm. "Flint created ugly, misshapen things," she continues in a soft low voice, "like scalping knives . . . and war."

"Flint was a bad man," Quetit whispers, gazing up into Nonschetto's eyes.

"Yes, little one, he was." Nonschetto smoothes the hair away from Quetit's face while a sad, knowing smile crosses hers.

"And Sapling was good, like God."

"I do not know this white man's word . . . 'god,'" Nonschetto says, flicking a fly off Quetit's shoulder.

"God made everything," Quetit explains. "The earth. The sky. The crickets. Tskinnak told me about Him. In the clearing where we gather garlic. Sometimes we sing a song to God. One Tskinnak's mother taught her."

I feel uncomfortable beneath Nonschetto's stare. I know I'm not supposed to be sharing the white man's God with Quetit. But He means life to me.

"I recall hearing of your god," Nonschetto finally says. "But it was long ago. Before the war. Now you must keep his white man's name only in your heart. Do not speak aloud of god. Not in this village."

"Tskinnak said that Tiger Claw would skin us," Quetit says.

"Anger at the white man has turned Tiger Claw bitter, like unripened fruit."

"Why?" Quetit asks.

Nonschetto starts to braid Quetit's hair. "The white man killed Tiger Claw's father," she says softly.

"In the war against General Braddock?" I ask.

"Before the war. The men were hunting. They returned to the campfire and were sharing a meal when they were attacked. The white man shot Tiger Claw's father, Kahonhes, in the back. Then he scalped him."

"The white man *scalped* him?" I ask, thinking of how much I've hated Tiger Claw for the two scalps he has taken.

"Yes. Woelfin mourned her husband's death for many moons. She had known Kahonhes since she was a child." Nonschetto finishes braiding Quetit's hair. She wraps dried grass around the ends.

So this is the briar that chokes Woelfin's path. I feel hurt, ashamed of what my people did. The white man *can* be as savage as the Indian. It is a troubling thought.

119

"*Why* did the white man kill Kahonhes?" I ask, needing a reason for the savagery.

Nonschetto shrugs. "Perhaps he was hunting too close to a white man's farm. It is hard to know."

Gokhas whimpers in my arms. I have been hugging him too tight. I kiss his round dark face and he nestles close to me. I realize with a pang how much he and Nonschetto mean to me. I would die if the white man hurt them.

Quetit fingers her braid. "Nonschetto. What happened to the Bad Twin? Did he die?"

"No, he did not die, for the Bad Twin creates evil and there is always evil in the world."

"And that's the end of the story?" Quetit asks, looking disappointed.

Nonschetto wraps her arms around Quetit and hugs her close. "No, Little One. It is the beginning. For the Good Twin needed someone to till the ground and make the corn grow strong. To stand by the man who hunts the deer, bear his children, and comfort him when the Bad Twin covers the sky with thunder clouds."

"So the Good Twin created woman," I say, finishing the story for Nonschetto, thinking of the comfort she has given me. Thinking of my mother . . . and Woelfin. All the women who must bear sorrow.

Nonschetto's answering smile touches me like the warm wind sighing through the trees. Now I understand why she chose this time to tell me about Kahonhes and the savage death he suffered.

Nonschetto's story of the woman falling through the sky reminds me of one I read in the Bible. It was about Eve, the mother of all people. I still can picture the words. Adam and Eve. The Garden of Eden. The evil serpent. Abel and his wicked brother, Cain. Since time began, Nonschetto's people, like my own, have had to explain why there is good and evil. Somehow, knowing this makes evil easier to bear. One day I must share Eve's story with Nonschetto. I think that she would like it.

Nonschetto nuzzles the back of Quetit's neck, where the skin is soft and pale. Quetit giggles. Gokhas croons as he pulls gently on my long black hair, then wraps his plump hand around my thumb. He closes his eyes. The sun glancing off his right cheek turns it into warm shades of copper.

Within the cool shade of the tall oak tree, we rest together now in a comfortable silence. Just the four of us and Tummaa. He is sleeping on his side—a plump gray puppy. He does not notice the butterfly hovering just above his nose. A fluttering of black and gold.

CHAPTER
Thirteen

The month of falling leaves has passed. Now Lowanachen, the North Wind, ruffles the tails of the busy squirrels. It carries the cries of geese throughout the land. I cannot listen to the geese without remembering my white man's home. Each spring and fall, the geese would fly through the sky above my cabin and I would run outside to watch and wonder where they flew. Twelve moons ago, the geese cried overhead when I stumbled over windfall and cut my feet on briars. The geese remind me of a long, sad journey and a home that I was forced to leave.

But I must not dwell in these sad thoughts, for now is the time of giving thanks for the bounty God has given us. Today, Indians from a nearby village come to share this bounty and dance in thanksgiving before their Lord, the Great Spirit.

I have already peeled the hickory nuts for the harvest feast. Now, with a mortar, I pound the kernels nesting in a gray stone bowl. As the kernels turn to powder, I add water to make a milky soup. The pottage I made earlier from dried corn and water steams in a kettle set over the fire. I wish these chores were finished. Everyone else seems to be getting ready for the celebration. I have no clothes to change into, but I'd like some time to grease my hair, tie it back with a strip of deerskin the way the other women do.

Men crouch in groups outside the sweat lodge preparing themselves for when the visitors arrive. I wince as I watch them intently pluck out hairs from each other's faces with wire tweezers. Once their faces are smooth and hairless, they will paint them. I am relieved that I am not a man. I would hate to have whiskers plucked out from my face.

I do not see the women anywhere. Like Woelfin, they are probably inside their huts changing into fancy clothes. I feel ashamed of this old dress I must wear. It is dirty and it smells.

I take the milk I have made from the powdered nuts and water and add it to the pottage. The mixture smells rich and filling. Mother once made a pottage like this for our Thanksgiving feast. Christian helped her roast the goose. I remember the sweet taste of the apple dumplings my sister made.

I wish I were home, sharing Thanksgiving in the warm circle of my family, instead of here, dreaming of nice clothes while I do chores in old ones. I pray for my family as I stir—my mother, my sister, my two brothers and my father—three of them scattered like leaves in the wind, two of them gone. But prayers do not ease the hard knot I feel where my heart should be. Some days, it burns inside me like an open wound.

"Tskinnak. I will watch the pottage now." Woelfin takes away my ladle and hands me a bowl. "Run quickly to Nonschetto. Ask her if I could have some vermillion, the red face paint."

I walk slowly to Nonschetto's hut, still lost in my sad thoughts. The wind brings the scent of roasting venison, the sounds of laughter. Tummaa scampers ahead of me. He attacks a pile of swirling leaves and barks at me, asking for attention. "Silly Tummaa. Come." I pat my side and he prances over to me. Tail held high.

Soft giggles greet me when I enter Nonschetto's hut. Heads turn—Woates, Flat Nose, Nonschetto and three other women. They are dressed in deerskin blouses and colored skirts of blanket cloth. Nonschetto wears silver brooches down the front of her blouse. Strings of little bells encircle her ankles. They make a tinkling sound as she approaches me. I have never seen her wear such finery.

"Tskinnak. Look at me!" Quetit dances out from the circle of women. Her eyelids and cheeks have been painted red. She wears a new blouse and a deep blue skirt.

"Where did you get the clothes?" I ask, wishing I had some too.

"Nonschetto gave them to me."

"Tskinnak. Do not look so sad," Nonschetto says.

"We have not forgotten you." She leads me to the women and they remove my ragged deerskin sacque. Nonschetto hands me a deerskin blouse and bright red skirt. For a moment, I hesitate, remembering a plain homespun dress Mother once made for me. What would Mother think of these Indian clothes?

"I traded fox pelts to get the blanket cloth," Nonschetto says. "Then I made the skirt in secret. So that I could surprise you."

I throw my arms around Nonschetto then, all hesitation gone. "The clothes you made are beautiful," I whisper.

Nonschetto rests her cheek against my hair and she hugs me back. The hard knot inside me loosens. Nonschetto, little Gokhas, Quetit and Tummaa are my family now. Tonight, when I say my prayers, I must give thanks for them.

I dress slowly, enjoying the feel of soft deerskin, the warm nap of the blanket cloth. Nonschetto is good to me. I must think of something to give her in return.

After I am dressed, Nonschetto paints my face. Flat Nose leans over her shoulder, giving her advice while Woates greases my hair, folds it back and ties it with a yellow ribbon. Quetit worms in between the women and stares at me. "You do not look like Tskinnak anymore," she says.

"Tskinnak looks like a woman," Nonschetto says with pride.

I am twelve winters old now. The top of my head

125

reaches Nonschetto's chin. Does that mean I am a woman now? I blush at the thought, for I feel like a girl.

"Look!" Woates says. She holds up a shiny piece of tin. "My husband, Gray Fox, bought this from a trader. You can see yourself in it!"

I stare at my reflection, made golden by the firelight. The redness of my painted cheeks and eyelids brings out the darkness of my eyes. My hair shines. Like folded blackbird's wings, it frames my heart-shaped face. Now I understand what Quetit said. I do not look like myself at all. I look like an Indian woman. This both pleases and disturbs me.

Nonschetto's gaily painted face smiles when I look up at her. And seeing the bright vermillion designs on her eyelids and her cheeks, I suddenly remember why Woelfin sent me here.

Tiger Claw comes out of our door flap as I hurry in with the vermillion Woelfin asked me to borrow from Nonschetto. Tiger Claw's face is painted to look like an eagle's. His forehead and neck are dead white. Dark paint outlines the ridges above his eyes. It shapes the yellow paint covering his nose and mouth into the cruel curve of a beak. His fierce eyes widen when he sees me.

I brush past him, afraid of his strangeness, the admiring look I see in his eyes. As the door flap closes between us, I try to make light of his look. Perhaps it is one of surprise at seeing me dressed up this way.

Woelfin sits on her bed, arranging a cloak of goose feathers around her shoulders. For many moons, her stiff hands have worked this cloak. Three strings of colored wampum now hang from her neck. She looks regal in her finery. Like an elegant, but distant queen. For a moment, I sense the beauty she must have been when she was young.

As I hand her the vermillion, I hear the tinkling of ankle bells, the shouting of loud halloos outside. The visitors are arriving.

"You are late," Woelfin says, her cold eyes staring into mine. "Quickly. Paint my face." Woelfin remains silent as I dab paint on her eyelids and cheeks. She says nothing about the way I look or where I got my clothes. Her silence makes me feel as plain as stone.

When we finally go outside, the sun is setting in bands of pink and gold. The men are kindling a fire in the village clearing. People are everywhere, greeting each other like old friends.

"Tskinnak," Woelfin says, gripping my arm. "You stay here and tend to the pottage. Do not let it burn." Then she hurries off.

I stir the pottage cooking on the spit outside our hut and watch Woelfin's feathered cloak move in and out among the people. I feel left out—all dressed up, but with no one to greet.

The visitors and the people of our village laugh and talk together as they enjoy the feast we have prepared. Their clothes, their painted faces, are like autumn leaves, coloring the village in cheerful reds, oranges, yellows and browns. Quetit races by me, chased by a gaggle of children I have never seen before. I am envious of Quetit. She makes friends so easily.

As night descends, Woelfin keeps me busy offering venison to the men and checking the pottage to make certain that it doesn't burn. I don't know why I'm wearing fancy clothes. This is just another day. At least sweet Tummaa stays beside me. My little watchdog.

Once everyone has eaten, the drum beats begin. The men join together, making a circle around the fire. Bells jingle as the women form a circle surrounding the men's. I add kindling to the small fire burning beneath the pottage, begrudging the task. But when the dance is over, people will want more to eat.

"Tskinnak." Nonschetto runs up to me, her ankle bells jingling. She takes my hand. "Come. Join us for the pipe-dance, the dance of friendship."

"But the pottage," I say, pulling back.

"Let the pottage cook itself! Come! The pipe-dance is fun and easy to learn. Just follow me."

Reluctantly, I let her place me in the women's circle. I feel shy and out of place between Nonschetto and the fat, dark-skinned woman who takes my other hand. The brass thimbles which decorate her skirt jingle as we slowly begin to dance. I watch Nonschetto's feet, imitating the steps she taught me moons ago. We step forward and back, moving counterclockwise to the drumbeat. The men dance in a circle formed inside of ours. The steps are easy. I begin to relax and let the drumbeats guide my feet.

One man, whose face is painted like that of a pike fish, starts to chant. He springs forward, breaking the line of the inner circle. He turns around several times, drawing the line of men around him until he is enclosed by them. Everyone chants as he now untwirls the line, leading the men in a snakelike chain. Tiger Claw brings up the rear, his fierce eyes aglow. I feel him watching me as I dance past. I watch my feet, afraid that I might stumble.

The fat woman releases my hand. I find myself being pulled along behind Nonschetto. Bodies press against mine as the fat woman draws us all together in a warm close chain of friendship. Quetit passes in front of me, her face flushed and happy. I like this dance, too. It makes me feel a part of everyone and they, a part of me.

We dance round and round, twirling and untwirling in a colorful, endless chain. My feet move to the beat of drums and chanting voices. We circle the bonfire, its bright flames flickering against the sky. I feel a part of fire and light. This dance makes me feel a part of everything that moves. I could dance like this forever.

Amid the rhythmic sounds of drums and ankle bells, there sounds a sudden loud halloo. I glance behind me. A wiry, dark-haired white man leads a bay horse into the village clearing. He halloos again. The drum beats cease and the dancing stops. I feel myself drop, abruptly, into the sudden silence.

"It is Dupré, the Frenchman," Nonschetto whispers.

"Why does he come now?" I ask, not wanting the happy dance to end.

"His custom is to join us in our harvest celebration."

"Children!" The Frenchman holds up two rifles. "I bring you greetings from your fathers, the French. I bring you guns, powder and lead. Enough to kill the English army!"

This Frenchman should not speak of war. Not now. This is meant to be a time of friendship. The men talk excitedly among themselves as they surround him. Tummaa crowds against my skirt and Quetit grabs my hand. We join the women who stand a respectful distance from the men, but close enough to overhear what they have to say. Tiger Claw greets the Frenchman like an old friend, clasping his shoulders, smiling his welcome.

"I have not forgotten you, my brother," Dupré says to Tiger Claw. He hands him the rifles.

So this is the trade Tiger Claw made with the Frenchman six moons ago. Furs for rifles to kill the English! But we need blanket cloth to keep us warm since Tiger Claw has sold off all his furs. We need hunting knives. The other day, Woelfin broke her blade while butchering a deer.

"Children. The French and Indian must allow no grass to grow upon the warpath leading to the English forts." Dupré takes out flasks from his saddlebags and hands them to the men. "Let the spirit of rum make us joyful while we plan our war against the Yengee devils."

I hate this Frenchman. It is a time for peace, for

giving thanks, and he gives the men hard drink that will turn them mean. He continues to talk of war—saying that Chief Towigh's warriors must join the French in battle. That the French and Indians are wiping the English off the face of the land. Suddenly, I find his narrow eyes staring into mine. Does he sense how much I hate him? I turn away, feeling the coldness of his stare on my unprotected back.

The harvest celebration goes on. But Dupré's talk, the rum he has given to the men, turns them ugly. The dance of friendship becomes a dance of war. The women stand together in small, hushed groups watching the men leap in circles around the fire. Hidden within the shadows of the surrounding trees, I watch, too. Now the men drive tomahawks into a post that has been fixed into the ground and curse the Yengee devils. I don't see Tiger Claw or Dupré anywhere. They probably went off together, plotting war.

Tummaa paws my skirt and whines. I lift him up and hug him, needing Tummaa's reassurance as much as he needs mine. How could a dance of peace turn so quickly into one of hate? These people are driven by an anger I cannot understand. Their savage dancing frightens me.

I wish that I could stay here, my back protected by the trees, but I suddenly realize that I have forgotten all about the pottage. Woelfin will be angry if I let it burn. I slip through the trees to the spit I erected a few yards from our hut and find that the pottage has cooked to a thick hard crust. I search the crowds for Woelfin.

131

Now I see her in her feathered cape standing along-side the fat woman who danced with me. Their faces are turned toward the dancing warriors who pretend they are in battle. The firelight glitters off their sweat-streaked bodies as they threaten to beat and stab and cut each other with their tomahawks and knives.

My heart beating, I lug the heavy kettle into the forest. I scrape the pottage out and feel relieved once the remains are hidden in the leaves.

The howls of the angry warriors send shivers down my spine. Clouds cover the moon and a cold wind bites my skin. I hang the empty kettle back on the spit, then run to the hut to fetch my deerskin cloak. Tummaa pads along beside me, silent and subdued. Time was when I wished this night would last forever. Now I wish that it would end.

CHAPTER
Fourteen

Our hut smells of stale sweat. Even the sweet grass I hung from the rafters cannot mask the sour scent. The fire smolders, giving little light. Outside the drums still beat as the war dance goes on. I kneel beside my bed and feel beneath it for the basket in which I store my deerskin cloak.

Beside me, Tummaa growls. I reach out to calm him and feel the hackles rise along his back. Something is not right in here. The air feels thick with body heat. Someone moves in the shadows behind me.

"Tiger Claw!" I gasp when I see his face, not a man's face, but an eagle's, all beak and eyes. His dark-rimmed eyes stare into mine.

"I . . . I came for my cloak," I tell him as I quickly stand. I sense he has been drinking. His eyes are unfocused, as if he sees, but does not see. He is unsteady on his feet.

"Tskinnak." Tiger Claw slurs my name. He throws his arm around my shoulders. I try to push him off, but he leans on me and traps me with his weight. His breath stinks of rum. Tummaa cowers beside me, whining.

"Dupré. Meet my white squaw," Tiger Claw says.

"I am not your white squaw," I say, searching frantically through the dark and smokey air for Dupré. I would hate to have him creep up on my back.

Dupré emerges from the shadowy corner near my bed. His face is narrow, like a ferret's. His thin dark beard does not hide the smirk I see on his face. "So this is the squaw you captured last fall." Dupré eyes me, up and down. "Your hunting was good."

"Let me go." I struggle against Tiger Claw, desperate to escape from these two men. They have been drinking in our hut. They must have been plotting war, sitting on *my* bed. I hate them. Hate the touch of Tiger Claw's bared chest against the new clothes Nonschetto made for me.

"This white squaw needs taming," Dupré says.

"I am not a white squaw!" I say, hating the words "white squaw." They demean me.

"Tskinnak is tame. She does what I say." Tiger Claw squeezes my shoulder warning me to be silent.

"Then I leave you to your pleasure," Dupré says. "Tomorrow we talk more." Wind whips into the hut as he opens the door flap. The fire's hot coals blaze and sputter. The door flap closes and they die down.

I feel my heart beat, loud in my chest. "Let me go."

"Tskinnak." Tiger Claw throws his other arm around

my shoulders and he hugs me. The other times when he was drinking, he only touched me with his eyes, never with his hands. But Woelfin was nearby then. I must get out of here.

I throw my weight against Tiger Claw. I push as hard as I can and he stumbles backward. I slip out of his arms and back away, slowly, feeling my way around the fire toward the door. Tummaa growls and presses his body against my legs.

"I didn't say you could leave," Tiger Claw says angrily. He lurches toward me.

Tummaa barks and bares his teeth.

"Move!" Tiger Claw kicks Tummaa out of the way. The puppy wails as he tumbles backward into an earthen pot.

"Tummaa!" I scream.

Tiger Claw kicks my puppy again and then again.

"No!" I throw myself in front of Tiger Claw. I grasp his arms and jerk him away from my little puppy.

Tiger Claw tries to shove me aside. I sink my teeth into his arm and bite down, hard. Tiger Claw bellows with rage. He grabs my hair, drags me to his bed and throws me down upon it. "I teach you to be good squaw," he says, slapping my face.

"I hate you!" I scream.

Tiger Claw hits my face over and over again. Hot, bright pain sears my eyes, my mouth.

Suddenly, he stops. His breath is heavy, thick with the smell of rum. I feel his body lower over mine. Now it pins me to the bed. "You be good squaw," he mumbles.

Blackness hovers over me. "No. No." I throw my aching head from side to side.

"Good squaw." He runs a hand across my shoulder, down my arm.

I want to die. I wish that I could die. Oh dear Lord, help me, give me strength. Desperate, I shove my hand into Tiger Claw's chin, snapping it away from me.

Tiger Claw forces my hand backward and pins it to the bed. He grabs my other hand and holds it, too. I cannot move.

Minutes pass. Long minutes filled with shadows and Tiger Claw's loud breathing. Tiger Claw wants to possess me as . . . as a man does a woman. I sense it now. I feel helpless and ashamed.

I sink down into the bed, wishing the saplings would break beneath me. Wishing the earth below would part and I would fall into an endless inner sky where Tiger Claw could never reach me.

I begin to sink into my vast imagined darkness and a low voice calls me back. "Drunken dog," it says. "You would take a girl against her will? Like a Yengee devil? You shame our people."

"Nonschetto," I whisper, my relief at being rescued turning me as limp as rags. I struggle to see her. Pain flashes through my head as I open my eyes. But . . . it is not Nonschetto's face I see before I drown in darkness. It . . . is Woelfin's.

136

The next thing I know is the warmth of a compress against my cheek. I slowly open my swollen eyelids. Pale light seeps through the cracks in our hut. It is morning.

"Tskinnak. Do you feel better now?" Nonschetto sits beside me on my bed, her round face filled with sweet concern. She is gently bathing my face.

"My head hurts," I whisper.

"My heart beats in sorrow for what happened to you."

"How . . . how did you know?"

"Woelfin told me. She knows we are like sisters. She said you needed me. I have been here all night long, helping her to nurse you. We were worried that you would not awaken."

"Woelfin nursed me?" I whisper.

"She bathed your face with wet leaves and held your hands when you cried out."

Nonschetto must sense my disbelief. She smoothes the hair away from my eyes and says, "Tskinnak. Woelfin is old and bitter, but she is a woman. She knows how you feel."

I lift my hands and stare at them. I think of all the times Woelfin scolded and threatened me, calling me a lazy child who is good for nothing. And yet . . . Woelfin held these hands. She saved me from her son.

"Tiger Claw," I whisper, remembering his painted face, how it hovered over me. I hate him and what he tried to do.

"Tiger Claw left at dawn with the Frenchman and several other warriors. They join the Shawnee and other Delawares who raid white man's farms. Before Tiger Claw left, Woelfin cursed him. She said maggots will breed inside his body. They will eat his flesh and he will die in agony if he ever takes a woman against her will."

"Woelfin cursed Tiger Claw?" I ask, unable to believe it.

"Woelfin said no Indian may take a woman who is not his wife. It is a matter of honor with our people that goes beyond the ties of a mother to her son."

A shadow moves on the bark wall a few inches from my head. Woelfin's shadow. She tends to something cooking on the fire. Her shadow reminds me of a bird with broad dark wings. Woelfin's wings kept me from falling into a shame that would have darkened all my days. I must thank her.

Nonschetto supports my shoulders as I struggle to sit up. Pain pounds through my head and I see stars before my vision clears. Quetit's small body is not curled up on her bed. "Where is Quetit?" I whisper the question, but the words ring loudly in my head. I am afraid of what might have happened to her.

"I took her to my hut after I found out what had happened to you. She was so tired and sleepy from the dance, she didn't even protest," Nonschetto says. "She sleeps with Gokhas now. The two are curled tight together, like little bear cubs."

My relief is fleeting, for now I see the worn straw

138

mat beside my bed where Tummaa always sleeps. The mat is empty, like my heart. Tears fill my eyes as I think of my little friend, of how he defended me.

I do not ask Nonschetto about Tummaa, for I am afraid to hear her answer. No animal could survive what Tiger Claw did to Tummaa. I believe Tiger Claw enjoys killing everything I love.

Nonschetto helps me to my feet. Through my tears I see Woelfin, draped in a deerskin cloak. She stirs something in a kettle sitting on the fire's hot embers. She sees me staring at her. She lifts her ladle and points to me. "Tskinnak. You must eat." There is a hint of tenderness in her voice that belies the stern look on her face.

Nonschetto supports my arm and walks beside me to the fire. I try to drink the broth that Woelfin gives me, but the broth is hot and my throat is tight. I want to thank Woelfin for what she's done, but she says nothing more to me and I find I cannot look at her. I feel ashamed by what Tiger Claw tried to do.

The hut appears the same, as if last night had never happened. And yet, something is different. At first I cannot pin it down. Then, slowly, I begin to see. It is just a little thing. The bearskin Woelfin always keeps upon her bed is now spread out upon the floor.

My head pounds as Nonschetto helps me walk slowly toward the bearskin and I try not to hope too hard. Something still and gray lies upon it. Tummaa.

The puppy tries to raise his head when I kneel beside him. He slowly thumps his tail in greeting. A splint, made from a piece of kindling and wrapped around with deerskin, holds a broken leg in place.

"Poor Tummaa. His leg is hurt." Nonschetto kneels and rubs his ears.

"Who mended his leg?" I ask, basking in the soft feel of Tummaa's tongue against my hand. *Tummaa is alive.*

"Woelfin," she replies. "I watched her. She is good with animals."

Tummaa laps at the broth I offer him and I turn to gaze at Woelfin. I know she has heard every word we've said, but she says nothing. Like a crone, she hovers over the kettle, stirring her soup. She has saved me from her son. She has mended my puppy's broken leg. I should thank her. But I don't know how, for she will not look at me. My words of thanks stick in my throat and I know now that I can never say them. Woelfin creates a space between us that is too wide to bridge.

"Tskinnak," Nonschetto says in a gentle voice. She is going to tell me something I do not want to hear. I can tell by her tone. "Dupré told Clear Sky of a French trader who arrives at the river forks in two days. He brings brass kettles, fine beads and broadcloth. Clear Sky wants me to help in bartering. I must leave. Clear Sky's furs are packed. He waits for me."

"Do not go."

"It will be the last time to trade before the snow flies. I will bring you back beads. You will look pretty in the necklace I will make from them." Nonschetto places something cold and smooth in my hand. Her bone-handled knife. "This will protect you while I am gone."

"I do not want your knife." I try to hand it back to her, thinking that if I do not take it, Nonschetto will stay.

Nonschetto cups my hands with hers. She gently closes my fingers around the knife handle. "Come. I will help you back to bed."

"No. I will stay with Tummaa." I lie down beside my puppy and curl myself around his warmness. I close my aching eyes and feel Nonschetto's hand, soft against my face.

"Please. Don't go," I whisper again, knowing that the words are useless. Nonschetto's duty is to be at her husband's side. I sink into darkness, but I do not sleep. Visions keep swirling through my mind. Now I see Dupré, his sly smile. I know that Nonschetto believes the French are good friends to the Indian. She claims that, unlike the English, the French treat the Indian with respect. But . . . Dupré called me "white squaw." He left me alone with Tiger Claw, knowing what might happen. "Do not trust the Frenchman," I finally think to tell Nonschetto.

No answer comes. I open my eyes. The door flap is closed on this empty hut. Nonschetto is gone.

CHAPTER
Fifteen

The day after Nonschetto left, the rain began. It has rained for four days now. Water puddles in one corner of our hut. I have had to move my bed closer to the fire to keep from getting wet. Smoke stings my eyes and makes my head ache. But I am better now. My eyelids are no longer swollen and I can see.

Bad things come in threes. I learned this when I was small, like Quetit. You stub a toe, cut a finger and then you wait for the third bad thing. It always happens, and only afterward can you relax, knowing that, for a little while, you'll be hurt no more. Two bad things have already happened. Tiger Claw attacked me and he broke Tummaa's leg. What is to be the third bad thing? Could I call it the storm which has blown the shingles off our roof?

Outside, the wind mounts, slashing the rain against our hut. Quetit and I sew by firelight while Woelfin sleeps. I hope that she does not awaken soon. The damp air makes her bones ache and she is more ill-tempered than a wounded bear.

"Tskinnak. Look." Quetit shows me the design she has been sewing in her deerskin square. A smattering of stars covers a brown expanse of sky.

"You must make your stitches small and even. Like you did with this one." I point to a star she has neatly stitched in red.

Quetit unthreads all but the red star design and begins anew. She is good with her hands and patient, the way I was when my mother taught me how to sew. I still can picture the words stamped on my first sampler—"God Bless This Home." It is strange how clearly I can picture these words, while the details of my home and family fade. It saddens me to think that this is happening, but perhaps it's better my mind works this way.

These deerskin squares are hard to work. The dyed porcupine quills we use are not like a needle and thread. I am pleased with Quetit's progress, pleased with my own creation—a picture of the woman falling through the sky. The woman holds her arms out in the shape of a cross. Birds fly under her arms, holding her aloft. I need to sew in the shapes of clouds, the outline of a mud turtle waiting for her, then I will give the picture to Nonschetto. I hope that she will like it.

I wonder where Nonschetto is. I hope she has found shelter from the rain and that her trading has been good. I feel so empty when she is gone. Especially now.

Tummaa sleeps at our feet while we sew bright quill designs of yellow, red and blue. His leg is slowly mending. When I see him hobble, I see Tiger Claw kicking him. I hope the wilderness swallows Tiger Claw. I hope he never returns from battle. That would be a good bad thing.

I create clouds of blue, a red and yellow earth. My picture is completed. The woman falls through the sky and a large mud turtle awaits her in a sea of blue. I sleep, dreaming of Nonschetto, her smile when she sees what I have made.

Bird song awakens me at dawn. Sunlight slants through the hole in the roof which the storm has made. It shines on Quetit's face. She opens her eyes and reaches toward the light, as if she could capture it and claim it for her own.

"Shhh," I whisper when her eyes meet mine. "Do not awaken the old she-bear." I glance at Woelfin who snores loudly on her bed.

Quetit giggles. She hops out of bed and together we quietly slip outside. The earth has been washed clean and the wet trees sparkle.

"Tskinnak. Look! Nonschetto's home is broken." Quetit points to an uprooted locust tree which leans against Nonschetto's hut. We hurry across the village clearing, skirting the black water puddled in the bonfire circle. Up close, I see that the locust has crashed into Nonschetto's roof and a large branch bars the door.

This is the third bad thing, I think. And it is not so bad. A tree can be moved. A hut can be repaired. Thorns scratch my hands as I try to pull the branch away. Quetit tries to help me, but the branch is too heavy for us to move. We need a hatchet to cut it into pieces.

"You would mend a roof that shelters no one while we sleep in puddles?" Woelfin says when we ask for the hatchet. "Soon our hut will be filled with water. Where then will we light our fire? Take the hatchet. Cut the tree bark and patch our roof first. Pusik! Move!"

I do not want to patch our roof. I want to mend Nonschetto's. Woelfin knows this and she is jealous. She has always been jealous of the closeness Nonschetto and I share except . . . when I was injured. I grab the hatchet and take my frustration out on trees, slicing the bark away in jagged sheets.

Soon the village comes alive as people emerge from their homes to clear away the branches that have fallen against their roofs and walls. Gokhotit sits astride his roof, two huts away from me. His strong hands work quickly, tearing off broken shingles. Gokhotit is not afraid of heights, but I am. They make me feel dizzy. I always fear that I will fall.

I stand on an upturned log so that I can reach our roof. One by one, Quetit hands me the sheets of bark and I piece them together, so that the sheets overlap, covering the hole in the roof which the wind has made. The work is slow and tedious and my arms ache with it.

By noon, the roof is finally patched to Woelfin's satisfaction. By noon, the others have finished patching their homes, too. Now Gokhotit, along with Gray Fox, Woates's husband, drags the locust tree away. It pleases me to see the tree removed. I hated the way its branches barred Nonschetto's door.

Outside our hut, a tired Quetit sprawls in the sunlight with Tummaa on a bed she's made with her deerskin draped over a pile of leaves. I carry our leftover bark to Nonschetto's hut. Gokhotit stands outside, his hands on his hips while he stares up at the roof. "This is an evil sign," he says, pointing to the gaping hole. "Bad spirits will enter the hut and there is no one inside to scare them away."

"Then we must mend the roof quickly, before they can enter," I say, finding it all too easy now to picture these bad spirits. There are three of them and they perch in the dark branches of the locust tree, flapping large and scaly wings. Their eyes burn red like Meesing's and they look hungry. I race back across the clearing, their frightful image giving wings to my feet.

I gather the remaining sheets of bark and the village dogs start howling. They race through the black puddles in the bonfire circle, their hackles raised. Tiger Claw has returned, I think, prickles dancing up and down my spine.

146

But Tiger Claw does not come out of the forest. Thistle does. And Clear Sky walks behind her. But I don't see Nonschetto. Maybe Clear Sky took her to her village, to visit with her sister, White Cloud. She didn't tell me she was going there.

I drop the load of bark and run to Clear Sky. "Where is Nonschetto?" I ask, suddenly afraid of the expression I see on his face.

Clear Sky stares at me, his face like a mask. He brushes past me and halloos. And as this mournful death cry echoes through the village, as the men, women and children hurry out of their huts, the third bad thing, larger and darker and more terrible than I could ever imagine, grips me in its talons and does not let me go.

Stunned, I listen as Clear Sky now tells the assembled people what happened to Nonschetto. Of how she stood at the cabin door while inside, Clear Sky bartered with the fur trader. How she held Gokhas in her arms. Suddenly, there was the sound of hoofbeats, of white man's talk. Nonschetto said something in the white man's tongue. Then rifles fired.

The awful shame, the horror I felt when Tiger Claw attacked me, cannot match what I am feeling now. I taught Nonschetto how to speak like a white man, but only a little. Did my words trigger the white man's gun? "Hello." "Do you have bread to eat?" "I trade four furs for one blanket." "I . . . love you."

Quetit runs over to me and, sobbing, burrows her face in my deerskin skirt. Quetit's hair is matted, full of

147

leaves. I pick them out, one by one; watch them flutter to the ground as Clear Sky tells how he buried Non-schetto with her feet toward the sunrise.

"The white man killed my wife, my son," Clear Sky is shouting now. "My blood cries for revenge!"

And in the hollowness that was my heart, I imagine all the bad things in this world flapping in the wind. They come together, folding their scaly wings, and form the figure of large dark evil man. He is as bleak as death.

"Tskinnak." Quetit pulls at my dress. She looks up at me, her face streaked with tears. "Clear Sky says Non-schetto has gone to *Assowajame,* the land beyond our sight. Can we go there too? Can we see Nonschetto? Tskinnak. Why did the white man shoot her?"

I brush past her, too filled with my own dark thoughts to answer. I wander aimlessly through the village and find myself outside Nonschetto's hut. No one has mended the roof, but it does not matter now. The bad spirits have already entered. The wind brings the smell of wet ashes. Gokhotit sweeps away the black water that has pooled within the bonfire circle. Gray Fox covers the wet ground with leaves and dry branches that have been stored within the lee of the sweat lodge.

Clear Sky lights the bonfire. I join the wailing women who surround the wet and smoking wood, Quetit cling-ing to me. The warriors begin to dance.

"The white man is evil," Woelfin says, her dark eyes wet with tears as her fingers clutch my arm. "He must die."

148

I pull away, hating the feel of her curled fingers. The warriors howl and Clear Sky raises his tomahawk. He curses the Yengee devils and drives the blade into a post.

The warriors' answering cries of revenge cut through me like a knife. Suddenly, I understand the savage anger that drives them to burn and pillage and I want to go to war alongside them. I want to kill the white man who shot Nonschetto—an eye for an eye, a tooth for a tooth.

And yet, just as clear and sudden as my anger, I hear my father's voice. "If anyone strikes you on the right cheek, turn to him the other also . . ." And I see my father more clearly than I have in many moons—his pale hands hang limply by his side while dark insistent ones search his clothes for weapons he has never owned.

Gray Fox flings his knife at the painted post. The knife point burrows into the wood, the blade quivering, reflecting the firelight, the awful confusion I am feeling.

I push past the women crowding around me. I run into the forest, blood pounding through my head. Brush pulls at my leggings, grabs my hair and I welcome the pain. Behind me, Quetit calls my name.

I push on, fording the stream where the tree was struck by lightning. Icy water soaks my moccasins. I scramble up a muddy bank and see the clearing in the trees. The clearing where I have prayed to God for strength. The clearing where I have sung praises to Him in the white man's tongue.

God, the white man has killed Nonschetto.

Grief as dark, as sudden as Nonschetto's death, envelops me. My chest pounds with pain, as if my very heart were breaking. I curl myself down into a ball and hug my knees. Wings are beating the air above me. Large, black wings. Now I feel them curl around me.

"Tskinnak?" It is Quetit's voice.

"Go away."

"Tskinnak. Hold me. Please."

I open my eyes. Something about the way she reaches out to me. Something about the loss and confusion I see written on her tear-stained face breaks through the blackness that is drowning me. I grab her outstretched hands as if they were my only lifeline. I enfold Quetit in my arms and we rock together, she and I, locked in sorrow.

"Alone, yet not alone am I, though in this solitude so drear . . ." I find myself singing my mother's hymn for Quetit. I sing it for me and for Nonschetto. Where is she now?

In the sky above, clouds drift like wind-blown feathers.

We are all but feathers.

Oh, God, please, be the wind.

CHAPTER
Sixteen

Tiger Claw returned in the month the trees crack with cold, one moon after Nonschetto died. I was skinning the carcass of a rabbit when he came through our door-flap. I stared at him, my hands red with rabbit blood, as was the knife I held—the hunting knife Nonschetto gave me.

Tiger Claw looked away before I did. He gave Woelfin two red blankets, a brass kettle he must have looted from a white man's cabin, a finely beaded belt and a promise of deer meat to see her through the winter. Woelfin was pleased with his offering. She did not scold him for his absence, nor remind him of what he tried to do to me.

But I have not forgotten and I never will. I go to sleep each night with Nonschetto's knife tucked in the folds of my deerskin blanket. Tiger Claw has watched me finger the sharp steel blade. He knows that I am not afraid to use it. Tummaa still sleeps by my bed. He is almost full-grown now. He is bigger and stronger than

Thistle, his mother. Tummaa bares his teeth whenever Tiger Claw comes near. Tiger Claw keeps to his side of the fire and we, to ours.

Clear Sky and his warriors returned soon after Tiger Claw. But seeing the two brown-haired scalps they took in revenge for Nonschetto's death gave me no pleasure. Scalps cannot bring Nonschetto back to me.

Nonschetto is gone and with her is buried all memories of my white man's home. It was not something that I wanted to happen. It just did, the way new skin covers wounds.

Quetit was watching Woates nurse her newborn son the morning I discovered what the shock of Nonschetto's death has done to me. It was during the month in which the ground squirrels begin to run. Quetit, her eyes wide with wonder, turned to me. "Tskinnak," she said, pointing to the baby. "Was I once small like this?"

"Yes," I replied, watching the baby's hand grasp his mother's thumb, the way that little Gokhas once clutched mine.

"Did I have a mother like Woates?"

"You had a mother and she held you the way Woates now holds her son."

"What did my mother look like?"

I shook my head. "Quetit, I never saw your mother. Perhaps she had light hair like yours." I ran my fingers through Quetit's hair, then stopped to unknot the dry and tangled ends.

"What did your mother look like?" Quetit asked, backing away from my attempt to comb her.

I tried to picture my mother then, wanting to give Quetit a sense of family, but I couldn't do it. An aching hurt filled the hollow of my heart, for all I could picture was an Indian burial ground with two fresh graves. "I don't remember my mother," I told Quetit.

"You must remember *something*," Quetit said.

I closed my eyes and with all my aching heart I tried. I saw a dark mist and two oxen pulling a wagon away from me. That was all. And suddenly, I felt so terribly alone, with nothing to fill the years behind me and nothing to look forward to.

"What do you see?" Quetit asked.

"Nothing." But recognizing the disappointment in Quetit's face, I said, "I once had a sister. She was like you—good with her hands and quick to learn. She was captured by Indians, too. I don't know where she is now, and I haven't thought about her in many moons, for it saddens me. I also had two brothers."

"And you had a father," Quetit said. "His hair was gray."

I did not need to ask her how she knew the color of my father's hair. Like me, she sees it every day, a dried and shrunken scalp hanging from the pole inside our hut.

But ever since that morning, I have dreamt about my mother. I am walking alone on a vast and treeless plain. Out of a distant mist, she approaches me. I cannot make out the details of her face, but her hair is the color of the hickory nut, once its rind is peeled. Her skin is like white willow leaves, pale and silky. She holds her arms out, as if she were waiting for me. I run across the plain toward my mother. I run on and on, the breath burning in my throat, but I never reach her. The seasons change, winter into spring and spring into summer, but the dream remains the same. It leaves me feeling tired and empty.

Now, on this hot and breathless day, when even the breeze is too tired to blow, I work in our garden patch, hoeing the corn the way I did last summer when Nonschetto was alive. But I do not feel the anticipation I felt then. No one waits for me beneath the oak tree.

A stone whizzes by my face. Quetit's small figure darts through the corn stalks, followed by three others. "You're supposed to hit the crows, not me!" I yell.

The corn stalks part and four children emerge, looking hot and dirty. "Tskinnak," Quetit says, planting herself in front of me. "It's too hot to throw stones at crows. We want to hear a story."

"I do not tell stories," I say, digging at a clump of thistle trying to crowd out my corn.

"I told you she didn't," Stone Face says.

"But she does," Quetit says. "Tskinnak used to tell them all the time before Nonschetto died. One was about the rain, a great canoe and a woman who fell through the sky and landed in it!"

"No, Quetit. You have mixed two stories together

and made them into one." I gingerly pull the thistle plant up by the roots and toss it aside.

"Then unmix them for me. Please?"

I lean on my hoe and stare at them: little Nunscheach, with the big dark eyes; Stone Face, his skin pitted with scars from an encounter with a porcupine; Running Water, whose mother gave her son this name because he can't stand still; Quetit. All their faces are filled with hope. I remember how I felt at their age when I was tired and bored and wanted something to look forward to. I can't refuse them the pleasure of a story.

"All right." I throw my hoe down. "The ground is too hard to work anyway."

Quetit squeals with delight. She and Running Water race over to the oak tree while Stone Face and Nunscheach take my hands and lead me to it.

And there, with Quetit's head pillowed on my lap, and Nunscheach leaning against my shoulder, I begin to tell the story about the woman falling through the sky.

"Once there was a land of happy people who lived above the sky," I say. "There was no sickness nor death in this land, for the Chieftan of the Skies who ruled it was good and kind. . . ."

As I repeat the words Nonschetto once said, I begin to feel as if she were beside me. I see her face in the little children's eyes, so bright, so filled with wonder. Tears sting my eyes as I spin her tale about the earth's creation, but I do not stop. For I sense that this might be the answer to my loneliness—to pass on all the stories Nonschetto told. It makes me feel a part of her.

When I am finished, Quetit snuggles in my arms. "Tell the other one now, about the great rain and the big canoe that holds all the animals."

I struggle in silence to find the beginning of this story, for my mind feels as if it were thick with weeds. "What was the old man's name?" I finally ask Quetit.

"Noah. You must remember Noah!" Quetit says impatiently.

"Noah." As I repeat the name, my mind begins to clear. "Once there lived a man named Noah. Noah was . . . six hundred years old when the flood of waters came upon the earth. It rained for forty days and forty nights." What joy I feel when I discover that I have not forgotten this story from the great book in which God speaks to man. As I tell it to the children in words they understand, I begin to feel as if my white man's family were beside me, too. It's not that I can picture them, but I feel their presence in my heart.

Even Running Water sits still as I tell of the old man Noah and his great canoe which will save the animals from the waters flooding the earth. I start to name the animals who board and Nunscheach places her hand on my mouth. "Let me name them," she says. In her thin, high voice, she sings out their names: the deer; the wildcat; the bear; and so on down to the little mouse, who burrows in the straw and squeaks.

"You forgot the crickets," Running Water says. "If the old man doesn't save the crickets, who will sing us to sleep at night?"

"And the owls. What about the owls?" Stone Face says.

They discuss which animals will board and a cooling breeze begins to blow. I lift my head to let it fan my neck and I see Woelfin standing under a nearby locust tree. How much has she heard?

Later, in our hut, Woelfin turns on me. "You poison our children with your white man's stories."

"These stories do not poison. They teach the children about the world and how to face both good and evil," I say, forcing myself to meet her gaze.

"These stories come from the evil ones."

"No," I say.

"They come from the people who shot Nonschetto."

I look beyond Woelfin to the scalp that hangs on a pole beside the door. "The Indian killed my father, but I tell the Indian's stories. Today, I told the children about the woman falling through the sky and later I will tell them about Meesing, Alcor and the three warriors who hunt for bear. They are good stories. But I will share others I remember, too." I pause, trying to think of them. "There is the tale of David," I say, suddenly re-membering. "He was a small but brave hunter who killed a giant three times his size. And . . . Daniel! He

157

was thrown into a den of wildcats and did not die." I take a deep breath, amazed at what I do remember, the strong feelings it evokes in me.

Woelfin slants her head and glances sideways at me, the way she often does when she is pondering. "This Daniel. Did he have a white man's gun?"

"No. The Great Spirit stopped the wildcats from devouring him."

"And the small hunter who killed the giant? What weapon did he carry?"

"A slingshot—the kind our children often use to kill squirrels and rabbits."

"Aaaiii! He was a brave man to kill a giant with a slingshot!" Woelfin brushes away a fly buzzing her face. "These people that you speak of, do they build their cabins on our hunting grounds?"

"No, they lived far away."

Woelfin shuffles to her bed and sits down. "Long ago, a wildcat attacked my son. Its claws were as sharp as hunting knives. Tiger Claw still carries the scars. You must tell him the story about Daniel."

"He would not listen," I say, hating the thought of talking to Tiger Claw at all.

"I once cursed my son to save you," she says, fingering the fringe on her deerskin blouse, then looking up at me. "Many moons have passed since then and he has not harmed you. You must open your heart to him."

"He does not open up his heart to me," I say bitterly,

thinking of the hurt he has inflicted on me and the heavy silences that now lay between us.

A beseeching look enters Woelfin's dark, hooded eyes. "Tiger Claw needs a wife to soften his hard edges," she says gently. "You know how to fish and plant and sew. You would be a good wife for him."

Time was when I would have welcomed Woelfin's words of praise. But not now. Not when they are linked to Tiger Claw. "I am only twelve winters old," I remind her, wanting to end the conversation.

"Soon you will be gathering milkweed floss to absorb your monthly flow. You will be a woman. Then we will talk more." She neatly folds the bearskin she's been keeping on her bed and tucks it in the basket where she stores winter clothes.

"Dreams haunt my sleep," I say, appealing to her superstitious side. "In my dreams, I always walk alone."

"Dreams change," Woelfin says mildly. "I will wait. Aiiii!" She fans her face. "It is too hot to move. Tskin-nak. Bring me water from the stream so that I may cool my feet."

The months pass—I turn into a woman. Woelfin sees me gather milkweed floss, but she does not mention marriage. I don't know if it's because she believes in dreams or because Tiger Claw is too often gone, fighting the war against the white man. Messengers often bring news of this war into the wilderness where our small village lies protected by hills and valleys thick with brush

159

and trees. They say the mighty Iroquois Nation has joined the French, the Delaware and Shawnee. One month, we hear that the English forts are toppling; the next, the French. I fear that soon all the rivers will run with blood. Even the friendly stream that winds through this wooded valley past my hut.

CHAPTER
Seventeen

I have lived in this village for three and one-half winters now. I have marked the passing of time with Nonschetto's hunting knife, carving small slashes in the willow tree that arches over the stream. I do not mark the days anymore, only moons.

The slashes remind me that I used to be someone other than Tskinnak, the blackbird. I can't remember the someone's name or from where she came, but sometimes I feel her wandering within the hollow of my heart, searching for a home. Sometimes I dream—seeing her run toward a woman with hair the color of the hickory nut. I wish dreams came true—that I could feel the warmth of a mother's arms surround me.

For three and one-half winters, the Indian has fought with the white man. Several of our warriors have died in battle and, along with other women in our village, I have mourned the sadness of their passing. But now, in this month of spring thaws, a new wind blows through our village. It sings a new song, a song of peace. This morning, a Delaware Indian I have never seen before rode a lean and lathered horse into our village. He said he was a messenger, sent by the English!

In front of all our warriors, he presented Chief Towigh with a belt of wampum which had two figures on it. One stood for the English, the other for the Indians of the Iroquois Nation and their nephews, us, the Delaware. The two figures were holding hands.

"Brothers of the Ohio region," the messenger began. "You see by this belt that we all stand together now, joined hand in hand. Men, you must bury your tomahawks in the ground, sit by your fires with your women and children and smoke your pipes in safety. Let the French fight their own battles. The Indian's war with the English is over."

I rejoiced at this happy news. Now husbands could stay with their wives and bring them meat and soft furs to clothe their bodies. Now fathers could be with their children. But Tiger Claw glowered at the messenger's proclamation. He dismissed the belts of wampum the messenger gave Chief Towigh with a disdainful shrug. I believe that war gives purpose to Tiger Claw's life. Without it, he has nothing.

Woelfin greeted the news with an impassive face. I'm certain she was disappointed that the English were triumphant. She hates the Yengee devils, who, she claims, unlike the French, want to possess all Indian land. Yet I'm also certain she was not sorry that bloodshed would soon end.

Quetit and I were not allowed to hear all the messenger had to say, for Woelfin saw us standing beyond the circle of the listening warriors and shooed us away, saying the messenger's words were not for our ears. That the fire was going out and we need wood to feed it. The weather has not yet turned warm.

But a strange excitement fills me as we now search for kindling. I heard the messenger say that this word of peace comes from Easton, a white man's town in Pennsylvania. A man of God brought this news to the Ohio region. A man named *Christian Frederick Post.*

In my mind, I picture this man of God. He is robed in white deerskin. He carries no guns to harm the Indians. The colors of sunrise surround his body and two morning doves perch upon his shoulders. He takes my hand and leads me toward the home whose warmth I've felt within my heart. And when we reach this home, the sun shines through the open door flap, setting aglow the figure of a woman who stands inside—*my mother.*

While the sun shines, glistening off the dark wet branches of the trees, I tell Quetit of my vision.

"Will the man of God take me with you?" she asks, the sunlight turning her hair to gold.

"You are my sister. Where I go, you go," I say. Quetit is almost seven winters old and has strong, sturdy legs. On this happy journey, I will not have to carry her.

"And Tummaa, can he go, too?"

Tummaa pricks his ears at the sound of his name and

163

ambles over to Quetit. She pats our large gray dog and he wags his feathery tail.

"Of course," I say. "We go nowhere without Tummaa. He is our friend."

"And Stone Face? And Nunscheach? Can they go too?"

"Their mothers are here and this village is their home. They would not want to leave it."

"But I would miss my friends." Quetit stares at the ground.

"I would miss them, too," I say, realizing the truth in the words. The children are a part of me and they have brought me joy. Yet . . . a longing tugs at my heart for something I used to know and love.

Quetit looks up at me. "Tskinnak. What does this home look like?"

I pause for a moment, trying to think how I can describe the feeling in my heart. "Home is always warm," I say, "as if five fires burned within it. I believe it has as many rooms as there are huts within our village, for it does not feel small and cramped like Woelfin's hut. Blankets colored in the shades of sunset must hang on the walls, for home feels rich with color."

Quetit slips her small hand into mine. "Tskinnak. If this is what your home is like, I want to go there, too. I hope the man of God comes soon."

And so we wait for this man to take us to the home and mother that I dream about. I do not forget Nonschetto and what she's meant to me. But I have not felt

164

a mother's arms in many moons. I believe that Nonschetto would understand.

Gradually, peace comes to our land. The men have time to hunt and fish and our bellies are full. The men trade furs with the English instead of the French and we have blankets to keep us warm. But it is an uneasy peace and I fear it cannot last. Too often the men complain that the English traders are too stingy with powder, bullets and guns. That they show no respect for the Indian and treat him like a dog.

One day, in the first autumn of this peace, with the leaves on the sugar tree red with frost, Tiger Claw returns from trading with disturbing news.

"The Yengee devils have betrayed us!" he tells Woelfin, the scar on his face turning white with anger. "They build a great fort at the river forks on the ruins of the French Fort Duquesne! They plan to house an army there! On land they promised to our people once the war with the French had ended!"

Woelfin's face pales, as if all the blood had been drained away. Quetit, Nunscheach and Stone Face, who have been playing the dice game with me in a patch of sunlight outside our hut, gaze wide-eyed at her and Tiger Claw.

I think of white man's guns, the bullets that killed Nonschetto. "You have said these river forks are a ten nights' walk from our village," I say, more to reassure myself and the little children than Tiger Claw or

Woelfin. "No white man's army will ever penetrate our wooded hills and valleys."

Woelfin turns to me, her eyes glittering with sunlight and anger. "You do not know the white man! No wilderness can stop him!" She pauses and I feel myself begin to wither beneath her gaze.

Tiger Claw grunts. He ducks through the door flap, carrying an armload of furs into the hut. The wind blows, scattering golden leaves through the village clearing. Stone Face gathers the black and yellow painted bones we use as dice and drops them, one by one, into the leather pouch he carries. He rises to leave and Woelfin stops him. "Stay," she says. "Listen to me." She crouches beside the children, her glittering eyes moving from Stone Face, to Nunscheach, to Quetit, then to me.

"Once, many winters ago," she says in the tone of voice we use for telling stories, "our people lived by the great waters. We gathered shellfish from the large green sea—sweet-tasting oysters, mussels and clams. There were many kinds of fish to eat. The land was rich. The corn grew tall and the deer were fat. We never hungered.

"But one day, the white man crossed the sea and beached his great canoe on our shores. He asked us for some land—no larger than the hide of the buck. He said that on this land he would build a fire to cook his food.

"We gave him land no larger than a buck hide, then watched as he took the hide, soaked it in water and cut it into cords! He tied the cords together. The land the long cord encompassed stretched from the deep green sea to the gentle hills and valleys.

"The white man repaid our kindness with trickery! But we kept our promise and let him keep the corded land. Sadly, we moved into the valleys where the sea breeze never blows. There we built our huts, planted corn and caught fish from the streams.

"The white man came to us again. He said, 'The land you gave us is too small. We choke on the smoke from the fires we kindle.'

"We said, 'We will give you more land on which to place your chair. There you will feel the warmth of fire but not its smoke.'

"Once more, we watched as the white man now unraveled the cords that formed the seat of his chair. He tied these cords together, too, and the long cord extended from the valleys to the mountains. We had been tricked again!

"We kept our promise. With sorrow in our hearts, we moved once more, across the mountains to these wooded valleys which are far from the sea breezes that we love. We built our huts, planted corn and fed the soil with fish heads.

"Now the white man comes again, for already he is building forts on land he promised to the Indian! Children! I tell you, the white man's cord will encircle our throats! He will tighten the cord with broken promises until we cannot breathe! Then, if we do not fight back

167

. . . we all will die." Woelfin's voice breaks as she says these words. Her eyes glitter now, not with anger, but with tears.

Someone begins to cry. I do not know who, for my eyes are locked on Woelfin's. For a moment, it's as if we touch, she and I. I *feel* the anguish at the white man's treachery that is reflected in her eyes. I feel her pain, and my heart aches.

Woelfin turns back to the children who wait. Nunscheach is sobbing. Stone Face clutches his bag of painted bones. Quetit strokes Tummaa, who rests his head upon her lap.

"Who can own the earth, the sky, the water?" Woelfin asks, waving her arm at the forest surrounding the village. "The Great Spirit has given them to us all! The Indian does not encompass the land with cords! He shares its goodness! The Indian does not rob the bee of all its honey! He does not kill for sport! But the white man does. And one day he will suffer for it."

Woelfin stands. She turns to leave us then, as if the sorrow that she feels is too great to speak of anymore. But her bowed back stiffens, straightens with pride as she enters her small log hut. I sense a grandeur in her. And I feel torn, for the first time, between two loyalties: one toward the Indian whom the white man has betrayed; the other, toward a dream.

The months pass, filled with disturbing news. English forts are springing up all over Indian territory: one at the Great Carrying Place; one at the river falls; and one at the land where the great lakes meet. As the English cord around us tightens, I greet each dawn with Tummaa, hoping that this day the man of God will come. And when he doesn't, I whisper the words to my mother's song. Sometimes they give me hope and the courage to go on. Sometimes they make me ache with a sadness that even Tummaa, with his antics, cannot heal.

And in the second autumn of this troubled time, Gokhotit returns to us after being gone for two moons. A wife walks behind him. She seems small and shy when, with downcast eyes, she is introduced to everyone. But at night, when our village celebrates the marriage with food and dance, her dark eyes flash with a fierce joy and her feet move like wings around the bonfire. Gokhotit calls her Proud One. It is a fitting name and I am happy he has found her. Her fire complements Gokhotit's sweet and gentle nature. Their marriage gives our village hope for future generations. There have been no babies here for many moons.

I watch Proud One dance with Woates, Quetit, Flat Nose and Nunscheach. The threat of war seems far away as golden leaves carpet the earth and the full moon turns the girls and women into dancing shadows. The air smells of burning hickory. Tummaa shoves his nose into my dress, asking for attention. I rub my hand along his flanks, enjoying the soft feel of his fur.

Beside me, Woelfin gossips with Mauwi, Chief Towigh's wife. I do not listen to what they say until Mauwi's shrewd dark eyes fasten onto mine. "Tskinnak," she says, gesturing toward Proud One who is joining hands with Quetit. "You must be sixteen winters old. It is time you marry, too."

"Aaaii!" Woelfin says. "This girl should have married moons ago. We need another man to provide us with bear meat and soft fur. We need children by our fire."

I am surprised at her words, for Woelfin hasn't talked of marriage for many moons. I thought she had forgotten it. But now I realize that having children in these troubled times would give her hope. "There are no single men here for me to marry," I say lightly, belying the sense of dread I feel. I do not want to marry. It would make me feel beholden to a husband. I am not ready for that. I don't know if I ever will be.

"Clear Sky needs a wife," Mauwi says.

"No," I say, shaking my head. "I could never marry the husband of Nonschetto."

"And there is Tiger Claw," Mauwi says.

"Tskinnak will have nothing to do with my son," Woelfin says. "He comes near her and she bares her teeth, like an angry dog."

As Woelfin speaks, Quetit dances over to me and grabs my hand. "Tskinnak. Come. Dance!"

I join the other women, relieved at being rescued. Instinctively my feet move lightly across the ground in time to the drumbeat. Tiger Claw dances with the men who form the circle inside of ours. His body is lean and hard, as are his eyes when he glances at me. Has Chief Towigh spoken to him as Mauwi spoke to me? I stare boldly back at him. He knows that I will never marry him, in spite of any compassion I might feel for Woelfin. I will kill myself before I do. When Tiger Claw leaves the next morning on a hunting trip, I rejoice.

In the days that follow the marriage celebration, Woelfin badgers me, saying, "It is time you took a husband. Tiger Claw needs a wife. This village needs babies."

"Gokhotit and Proud One will give you babies," I say, refusing to meet her gaze.

I dread Tiger Claw's return. In the clearing, with Quetit and Tummaa by my side, I kneel and pray, "Dear Lord. I am poor in spirit. Give me courage. If it be thy will, find a wife for Tiger Claw. Let Woelfin find contentment in the babies *they* will have."

The Lord listens to my prayers. I know He does. One moon after Gokhotit's marriage, Tiger Claw returns home with three deerskins and a wife! Oh how I rejoice when I meet her! She is from the Wolf Clan and Tiger Claw calls her No Thought. She is plump and soft, with small vacant eyes that are set too close together in her round face.

No Thought has earned her name. She builds fires, then gives no thought to tending them. She fetches water, then forgets the reason why. Quetit and I help her with her chores. No Thought is sweet and docile. The right side of her head is scarred. A drunken warrior beat her with a club when she was but a child. When Woelfin scolds her, No Thought fingers this scar and stares at the ground. I feel sorry for her.

I shield No Thought from Woelfin's scolding as I wait patiently for the man of God. But he never comes. And now our men grow restless, complaining that the English continue to betray the terms of peace. They build their forts and cabins on the Indian's hunting grounds and frighten all the game away. The cord that Woelfin spoke of is tightening around our throats.

The dark clouds of war gather overhead. And in this angry breathless time, Tiger Claw sharpens his knife and tomahawk, while at night, a recurring dream haunts my sleep. The man of God is guiding me through a forest thick with briars toward a vision only he can see. We travel on and on and my legs grow weary. I finally slump on the ground while the man of God moves on without me. And lying on that cold wet ground, I dream a dream within a dream. I dream of my mother, holding out her arms.

CHAPTER
Eighteen

Black flies circle overhead as Quetit and I boil deer brains in a kettle set above a blazing fire. When the brains are cooked, we will use the mixture for tanning hides. It is a hot and smelly job. We both hate it.

Achgook gave Woelfin this deer two nights before he traveled north with our warriors. After four winters of an uneasy peace, they join an Ottawa Chief named Pontiac. He is uniting the tribes in this wilderness. Together they plan to attack the English forts near the place where the lakes meet and kill the unsuspecting Yengees.

I wish that I could slip into the forest, where the air smells green. But Woelfin watches me, making certain that I finish this mean task. She punishes me by making me boil deer brains—a job saved for children who have misbehaved. Two nights ago, Achgook brought me this deer as a marriage gift and I refused it.

Achgook is short and stout. Although he only came to live in our village two winters ago, I know him too well. He thinks only of himself. His first wife died in childbirth at the time the frogs begin to croak. As soon as Achgook buried her and the baby, he began to notice me. When I see Achgook's thick, heavy hands, I am reminded of Tiger Claw and how his hands hurt me that dark night seven winters ago. I do not want to marry any man.

But Woelfin accepted the deer Achgook brought in spite of my protests. She said, "Achgook. When you return from war, Tskinnak will build your fire and grease your joints with oil."

"I will not marry Achgook," I told her later, stiffening myself to meet her gaze. "In my dreams, I walk through an endless forest and I walk alone."

Woelfin stared at me with eyes as hard as jasper. "This marriage has nothing to do with dreams. Achgook will hunt the deer for us. He will provide the fur we need. You will have children and their laughter will fill this empty village. This time, you *must* marry."

I add more deer brains to the pot and Quetit complains, making faces at me.

"Do not look at the brains, just stir them," I say, drying my skin with a handful of leaves.

"Tskinnak. My belly feels sick and I am thirsty." She hands me her ladle and slips away toward the stream. Knowing Quetit, her drink will be a long one. I cannot blame her. This is my punishment, not hers.

I look around me—at this village where I have lived for eight winters. It feels empty with our warriors gone. Woates sings a low sad melody as she sits outside her hut, grinding corn in a wooden mortar. Her only son died last winter from the coughing sickness and now her husband Gray Fox walks the warpath. She looks lonely without him. In the time of peace, he rarely left her side.

I am sick of boiling deer brains, sick of the thought of marriage and of war. In peace, I had discovered a measure of contentment sharing stories at the oak tree with the children. In peace, I could believe in dreams; imagine the warmth of my childhood home and a mother's arms. But war leaves no time for dreaming. War means clubbing mice to fill empty bellies. It means tending warriors' wounds and mourning those who've died. War is like a vulture, feeding on the dead. I don't know what has happened to the man of God. Did he go to Assowajame?

Two moons pass and the warriors return. Now Achgook struts through my garden as I try to hoe the corn. He boasts of victories against the English. Using his stubby fingers as counting sticks, he lists the forts the Indians have captured—Fort Sandusky, Fort Venango, Fort Miamis, Fort Le Boeuf . . . His loud boasting drives me away. Even Woelfin's threats cannot make me go near him.

Achgook and the warriors leave once more. This time for a place called Bushy Run. Two moons later, only five of them return—Achgook, Clear Sky, Gokhotit, Tiger Claw and Gray Fox. Achgook and Tiger Claw boast of the six Yengee devils they have killed. But Clear Sky tells us of a battle lost to a white man's army led by a chief named Colonel Bouquet. Eight of our warriors died in battle, as did many of the Seneca and Shawnee who fought beside them.

Our rivers run with blood, but the fighting does not cease. Our warriors join the Tuscarora. In small packs, they attack the cabins the white man raised on Indian hunting grounds along the Muskingum River. When cold cracks the trees, the warriors will return. Snow will fall. Food will be scarce. Our bellies will ache with hunger and Achgook will stand in our door flap offering gifts of deer and bear meat. How then, will I refuse him?

Now, in the month of falling leaves, bucks with polished antlers and swollen necks search for does. At night, I hear them calling for their mates. At night, Tiger Claw, Clear Sky and Gokhotit return. They lead a white man's horse into our village. Achgook's body, along with Gray Fox's, is draped across its back.

I treated Achgook badly. I never let him near me. But I did not want the white man to shoot him. I did not want him to return like this, as cold as winter stone. I feel the weight of this stone, as if it hung from a cord around my neck—choking me.

At daybreak, I help Woelfin prepare Achgook's body for the burial. We dress him in soft deerskin leggings and a broadcloth shirt we found folded underneath his bed.

"Achgook was a brave warrior." Woelfin's stiff hands

shake as she places a string of beads around Achgook's neck. "You should have married him."

I slip new moccasins that I have made on Achgook's feet, not knowing how to answer her, but feeling the familiar burden of guilt and sorrow settle on my shoulders.

"Achgook's spirit will not rest, knowing that you scorned him."

The people of our village observe a mourning silence before Achgook and Gray Fox are lowered in their graves. No Thought's new baby wails, breaking the silence with his hunger. No Thought takes him to her breast. Tiger Claw watches, impassive. While the baby nurses, we commune with the dead.

If I had married Achgook, would he still be alive? At night, I will throw fat upon the fire and the smoke will feed his spirit. The smoke will let him know I meant no harm. Will smoke erase the guilt I feel?

Woates, Gray Fox's wife, shrieks as her husband's body is now lowered in the ground. "Gray Fox. Do not leave me!" she cries, tearing at her hair, her dress. We join her in loud wails of mourning.

Through the days that follow this sad burial, I throw fat upon the fire. Achgook's spirit must be at rest. I do not sense his presence here. But the loss of Gray Fox haunts his wife. Each night, Woates places a kettle of food upon his grave. A silent sickness feeds on Woates. I bring her pottage, but she will not eat.

Before the snow flies, Woates joins her husband and I fear this is the beginning of the end. The white man's cord has choked us. We have no fine clothes to dress her body in nor kettles of food to place upon her grave. We have eaten summer's fruits and they are gone. We have little meat, for the men have had no time to hunt. We have no furs to trade for the guns, ammunition, knives and blankets that we need. And even if we had these furs, there is no one with whom we can barter. The English drove the French traders from our land and we cannot barter with the English. We are at war with them.

The sky is as gray as lead. The air is thick with the smell of snow. Tiger Claw, Clear Sky and Gokhotit, who brought the cold bodies of Achgook and Gray Fox into our village then stayed to mourn their passing, prepare to leave us now. "We travel north to speak with the Frenchman," Clear Sky says. "We must convince him to join Pontiac in the war against the English. When the leaves are green, the French and Indian will attack and finally defeat the Yengees at Fort Detroit. Then we will return to you in triumph, bringing the guns and knives and blankets that you need."

They depart, and the snow begins. We hole up in our hut like mice in straw—Quetit, Woelfin, No Thought, her baby, Tummaa and me. Outside the snow falls silently for two long nights. We eat a rabbit Tiger Claw trapped before he left and chew on the bones. My stomach cramps with hunger as I suck the marrow from the backbone. I find it hard to sleep.

On the third morning, the sun breaks through the clouds and melts the snow's white face. Oh, how we rejoice! Quetit, No Thought and I wade through the snow to visit with others. We share our hope for catching rabbits and wild turkey once the snow has thawed.

By night, the biting cold returns. The next day, I discover with alarm that the top layer of snow has frozen into a thick hard crust. I cannot hunt in it! My feet break through the crust and make loud noises which frighten all the game away.

I strap in my stomach to ease its cramping and anxiously wait for a thaw that does not come. Quetit and I try to gather bark from the sugar tree to eat, but the snow is too deep and the crust, too hard. It cuts into our legs and makes them bleed.

Desperate for food, I lead No Thought and Quetit through deep snowdrifts, searching for the deer bones we had thrown outside our hut in the peaceful days when deer were plenty. I boil the handful that we find and everyone drinks the broth. For a moment, the gnawing in my stomach eases.

All too soon the broth is gone. Two more nights pass filled with hunger. Quetit's eyes grow large in her thin face. Tummaa grows old overnight, gray bones and sweet brown eyes. But Woelfin stays the same, thin and hard. I wonder, if I had married Achgook, would we hunger now?

On the morning of the seventh day, Chief Towigh enters our hut. He is the only man left in our village and he is old and feeble. But now a strange light gleams in his watery eyes. "I have had a dream," he tells us. "A black bear sleeps in the hollow of an oak tree. I know this dead oak, as big around as five large bears. It stands where the stream divides in two, a one night's walk from here. In my dream, I saw bear knuckles strung around my neck. My belly was full."

"Follow this dream," Woelfin says, licking her lips. The thought of bear meat makes my mouth water, too. I have known hunger, but never like this—bone deep.

The sky is gray. A bitter wind tears at Chief Towigh's deerskin cloak as the women and children in our village watch him leave, carrying the only gun that we have left. He slowly walks through waist-deep snow, hunting the bear whose sleep is not disturbed by the sound of footsteps. I wish him a fruitful journey and a safe return.

Dreams are all we have to feed us while we wait for him. At night, in our small corner of the hut, Quetit and I pray quietly together while No Thought and Woelfin rock with hunger. No Thought's baby wails.

"The Lord will keep you from all evil," I whisper to Quetit. "He will keep your life. The Lord will keep your going out and your coming in." I see these words as clearly as I see Quetit's face. Through many winters, I have kept the Lord's words in my mind, like stitches quilled in deerskin.

Quetit holds my hand. Her blue eyes shine with love. Our prayers give us strength and we hold fast to them.

Through the nights, death stalks us. I hear him moaning through the trees outside. I feel his breath as I stumble through snowbanks, my fingers blue and frozen as I break through the crust trying to find a bone, something to boil in water. I crave the taste of meat. No Thought's baby grows pale and silent. She continues to nurse him, but her breasts are empty. I am afraid that he will die.

Three nights pass, then four, before Chief Towigh finally returns. Everyone gathers in his hut to hear what he has to say—Mauwi, Proud One with her baby boy, Flat Nose, Stone Face, Running Water, Nunscheach and Otter Woman with her three small children. Chief Towigh's lips are blue with cold, his wrinkled skin is gray. "The snow in the forest was as high as this." He points to his chest. His hands are calloused, gnarled like bark. "The crust cut into my legs like hunting knives." He pauses.

We hang on his pause, gazing hungrily at his empty hands.

"One night it snowed. I slept inside a hollow tree. The next day, travel was hard and slow. By nightfall, I found the dead oak and lit a fire beneath it. A large black bear, his sleep broken by the heat of fire and smoke, climbed out."

"Old man. Where is this bear? Does he live only in your dream?" Woelfin asks.

A weary smile lights Chief Towigh's face. "Old woman. The bear meat waits for you outside, behind this hut. I made a sled out of branches and brought back all the meat that it would carry."

Woelfin's eyes widen, reflecting her wonder and her disbelief. I know just how she is feeling. This bear meat is like the miracle of sunlight after many cold and bitter nights.

Mauwi and Woelfin roast the meat and we devour it like hungry wolves. I make certain Quetit and Tummaa get their share. The fat is sweet. It makes us strong. Milk begins to flow through No Thought's breasts. As I watch her nurse her son, I feel a kinship with her, with all the people gathered here. We have suffered. Most of our men have died in battle and we have hovered on starvation's biting edge. But Chief Towigh's gift of bear meat gives us life and, with it, hope. This snow cannot last.

CHAPTER
Nineteen

The people of our village have banded together. We are like one family with Chief Towigh as our father. Warm winds finally thaw the crusted snow, and we share the rabbits that we snare, the sweet sap that we tap from the sugar trees. When the leaves on the oak tree are the size of a mouse's ear, we sing softly as we plant our corn and wait—one man, seven women and nine children—for Tiger Claw, Clear Sky and Gokhotit to return. But the men do not come back. At night, seated around a council fire, we talk together and dream of better times when the loud talk of men will fill our huts and deer will hang once more from the drying racks.

Now, in the month in which the honey bees swarm, Quetit, Nunscheach and I harvest blackberries. The bleak winter months seem far away as we pluck plump berries warmed by the sun. Black juice stains our hands and a sweet taste fills our mouths.

Quetit's and Nunscheach's baskets are only half-full,

but now they sprawl together in a patch of sunlight, plopping ripe berries into each other's mouths. Tummaa lies beside Quetit, licking her face. She giggles and pushes him away. I wish I could lie down and enjoy the sunlight with them, but I know winter lies ahead. I must prepare for it.

Thorns scratch my arms as I stretch to pluck the ripened berries. Why is it that the big ones always hang beyond my reach? Something rustles through the grass. A black snake slithers across my feet. I leap backward, startled.

"Tskinnak," Quetit whispers.

"What?" I call, my hands trembling from the close encounter with a snake. I know black snakes are harmless, but all snakes frighten me.

Quetit runs over to me, followed by Nunscheach. "We hear footsteps," she whispers. "They come from there." Quetit points toward the thick stand of locusts that lines the footpath leading to our village.

"Who comes this time of year?" I say.

"I hope it is a trader," Nunscheach says. "I would like a string of wampum, pink and white, like apple blossoms."

"You had better hope for blankets and ammunition. Come. Let's see this trader." We slip into the woods and quietly move from the shelter of one tree to another. We crouch behind a pile of brush that overlooks the footpath. Tummaa wiggles between us, poking his nose into our faces. Suddenly, his hackles rise along his back. Tummaa starts to growl. "Shhh." I fold my hand around his mouth, silencing him.

Five figures slowly round the bend in the footpath. I strain my eyes, trying to see. "Who is it?"

"Tiger Claw." Quetit points to a figure who leans heavily upon another. "And that, that is Clear Sky! The third must be Gokhotit. I do not know the others. Come." Tummaa barks and bounds ahead of Nunscheach and Quetit as they race to the village. I walk slowly behind them, carrying our baskets and hoping that the men have brought the provisions that we need.

When Tiger Claw, Clear Sky and Gokhotit left last winter to speak with the Frenchman, they departed in hope. But now, as they stand in the village clearing surrounded by our people, my heart sinks, for their faces are lined with despair and their hands are empty, save for some worn gray blankets.

I do not know the Delaware warrior who stands beside them, dressed in buckskin leggings and a torn red shirt. But I recognize the fifth man. It is Dupré. He has aged. Has it been four winters since he last came here? Or has it been five? His beard is gray. He wears a stained buckskin coat fringed with horsehair.

"So, Tiger Claw. You still own the white squaw," Dupré says as I approach. His eyes remind me of a ferret's. They squint at me while a smile tugs at the corners of his mouth. "Have you found her a husband yet?"

Tiger Claw drapes his arm across Clear Sky's shoulder and spits on the ground. "What man would marry Tskinnak? Her nose is too big and her face, long like a horse."

I had eagerly anticipated Tiger Claw's return, the provisions he would bring. But now, stung by his ugly words, I suddenly wish he had never come back. "Where are the guns you promised us? The knives and the sweet talk of triumph?" I ask, wanting to wound him as he has me.

"The Frenchman would not join us in our cause. Without his guns and warriors, there is no hope," Clear Sky answers calmly, ignoring the sharpness in my retort.

"Pontiac's war is over?" Chief Towigh's voice trembles with the question.

"It is over." Clear Sky hands him three blankets. "We found these at an abandoned white man's camp. We thought you could use them."

"What good are blankets in this heat?" Woelfin says, her sharp eyes assessing Tiger Claw. I notice then how pale he is.

Tiger Claw grabs a blanket and wraps it around his shoulders. "They ease the chill of sickness. Where is my wife? My son? Why are they not here to greet me?"

"No Thought gathers sweet grass and berries," Woelfin says, placing a hand on Tiger Claw's cheek. He brushes her hand away.

"I will find No Thought," I say, wanting to get away from Tiger Claw and Dupré. Their presence reminds me of an ugliness I do not want to think of.

"Tell No Thought to bring me white willow bark," Woelfin says. "My son burns with fever."

During the hot days that follow Tiger Claw's return, his sickness worsens and we spend our waking moments nursing him. He complains that his body aches and No Thought rubs his joints with oil. He thrashes in the heat of fever and Woelfin brews willow bark to make a soothing tea. When Tiger Claw shakes with chills, Chief Towigh covers him with deer skins and the men place him on a pallet made of hemp and carry him to the sweat lodge where fire, water, steaming stones and Chief Towigh's incantations are supposed to make strong magic that will drive the evil spirits out of Tiger Claw and make him well. But when he returns from sweating, he is even weaker than before.

The rank smell of sickness continues to fill our hut. Red and angry-looking pox start to erupt on Tiger Claw's face and body. Quetit and I gather the fernlike leaves of the kinnikinnick tree. We boil them into a soothing medicine that No Thought and Woelfin use to cleanse and purify the festering sores on Tiger Claw's skin. I pray that the kinnikinnick leaves will ease his suffering, but ugly memories, like a gray scalp hanging in our hut, stand in the way of my compassion. I cannot make myself go near his bed.

Like Tiger Claw, Clear Sky sickens and then Atank, the Delaware warrior who returned with them. Dupré stays in a hut by himself. He says he does not want to catch this sickness. Once the leaves turn, he will travel

187

south, to trade with the Shawnee. I will be glad when he is gone.

When the sores on Tiger Claw's face and body begin to bleed, Dupré quickly packs his deerskin bag. "Tiger Claw has the smallpox. It is a white man's disease," Dupré tells Woelfin, keeping his distance. "Burn the blankets found at the white man's camp. They have been cursed."

The war has not ceased. It never will. Dupré walks away from us, his thin dark body disappearing into the trees and Woelfin wails, echoing the hurt and anger that I feel. I help her burn the blankets, but it is too late. A sickle moon shines the night Tiger Claw dies. "Aaaiigh!" Woelfin screams. All night Woelfin and No Thought grieve. Quetit and I grieve with them, for Tiger Claw's long suffering and this awful curse the white man has placed upon us.

Now the moon grows full and smallpox rages through our village. We have no breath left to mourn the dead, there are so many: Clear Sky, Gokhotit, Atank, No Thought, No Thought's baby, Nunscheach. Sometimes at night I think I hear her. A warm wind sings her melody, so high and sweet. I am afraid of who might sicken next.

CHAPTER
Twenty

A flock of hungry blackbirds perches in the oak tree. Their small hard eyes watch me as I hoe the corn. I scream and wave my arms at them. They fly away, harsh cries and dark wings swooping through the air.

Tummaa mumbles, as if asking, "What is all this fuss?" He shoves his graying muzzle into my deerskin skirt and I rub his ears. Tummaa sighs. I throw down my hoe and wrap my arms around him. He licks my face, trying to tell me, "Everything will be all right."

I wish I could curl into the shade with Tummaa and go to sleep. But I must dig out the weeds which choke the corn. It is a lonely, endless task without the other women hoeing beside me, passing time with song and gossip. And I don't know who will be here to harvest the ripened ears. Like the hungry blackbird, death perches in the rafters of our huts. Quetit has the smallpox now.

The squash I planted beneath the corn has withered.

The white grub has sucked it dry. Deer flies circle overhead and the air is thick with heat.

At noon, I stumble through the corn, back to Quetit, hoping that when I see her she'll sit up in bed and say, "I'm feeling better now."

The village is quiet. A lone dog rolls in the dusty ground outside Clear Sky's empty hut. Dust coats the two canoes upturned by the sweat lodge. I long for the sounds that are now missing: women singing as they hoe the corn and gather firewood; the rasping sound of men sharpening their hunting knives. It feels as if everyone has died. Even the birds are silent.

Shadows cast by the smokey fire greet me in our hut. Woelfin hovers over Quetit's bed, a bowl held in her hand.

"Is she better?" I ask, kneeling beside the bed.

Woelfin shakes her head. "The sickness breeds within her throat. She cannot drink."

"Tskinnak," Quetit whispers, reaching out to me. I take her hand, forcing myself to look at her face. The pox have begun to blister her skin, turning it red and raw.

"You must drink the willow tea," I say, carefully fingering away the hair sticking to the sores on her face.

"It hurts to drink."

"You must try."

"Not now, Tskinnak. Please."

"Perhaps you can drink later," Woelfin says. "It will make you strong. In here." She places her hand on

Quetit's chest. Woelfin's fingers curl from the old peo-ple's disease. Her long nails yellow with age. But I know now that this gnarled hand can be a warm and caring one.

Woelfin's deerskin dress brushes against my arm. I feel her fingers lightly touch my hair before she turns away.

The two dolls Quetit made from twigs and deerskin lie at the foot of her bed. I hand them to her now. "Remember the house game you used to play?"

Quetit hugs the dolls to her chest. "I made mazes in the mud," she whispers. "Nunscheach and I moved the dolls through the mazes until they found their home. But, Tskinnak. The mother doll you made from corn husks, the one who always waited for them, fell apart."

"You could have made another one."

"No. Only you can make the mother doll. Will you make one for me now?" she says, her voice a little stronger. "You and I can play."

"I will make one for you."

The corn has not yet ripened and the husks from the year before have rotted. I make a mother doll for Quetit from the dried sweet grass that hangs from the rafters in our hut. I twist the strands together to form the body, legs and arms, and dress the doll in a scrap of deerskin. But the doll is not the same. And the mazes that I make for Quetit in her blankets hold no secrets. I know where they lead.

The next morning, Quetit awakens caught in the

191

awful chill of fever. Woelfin, Chief Towigh, Mauwi and Proud One help me carry her on the pallet that was made for Tiger Claw into the dome-shaped sweat lodge. There we build a fire with twelve hardwood logs and place twelve stones upon the fire. When the stones are hot, we throw water on them, causing them to steam. Chief Towigh chants amidst the steam, beseeching the Great Spirit to drive the sickness out of Quetit. I hold her hand, feeling the weariness in Chief Towigh's voice, knowing his despair.

For a short time, the fever within Quetit seems to die down and she sits up in bed, chattering the way she used to. But then, as the afternoon sun beats down on our hut, new pox break out on her face and body and the fever returns. I bathe Quetit with the medicine made from the kinnikinnick leaves until she cries out for me to stop. And then, as she tosses in a restless, pain-filled sleep, I hover over her, feeling light and hollow, like the wing bone of a bird.

I know that it's wrong to question God's will, but I question it now. Lord, you must not allow Quetit to suffer this way. She is good and kind and gentle. Heal my little sister. Make her well.

The Lord does not answer me. I continue to nurse Quetit through the night and she grows weaker. Anger, like a thunder cloud, begins to brew in me: anger against the white man; anger against God. I feel like screaming, "We have done nothing to deserve this curse! We should not be abandoned this way!"

The next morning, Stone Face dies from the smallpox and then Running Water. I feel as if the whole world were crumbling at my feet. Quetit's eyes, once sunlight on water, are now but dried-up pools. I know that she is next.

Perhaps I can bargain with God. Tell Him, "Lord, if you would spare Quetit, I will devote my life to you." But I find it difficult to bargain with a presence I cannot feel. This must be what Hell is like.

In spite of the heat, Woelfin and I keep the fire burning in our hut both day and night. The smoke keeps the mosquitoes and the wolves at bay. Outside, the wolves howl all night long. They must scent this awful sickness. I am afraid they herald death.

Although Tummaa grumbles every morning, begging me to greet the dawn with him, I remain with Quetit. I dare not leave her anymore. When her face is slick with sweat and she is dulled by fever, I pray aloud for her. Woelfin grumbles when she hears these white man's prayers, but she does not stop nor punish me. I don't know if God hears them, but often, a smile crosses Quetit's face, as if she understands. "Dear Lord," I pray, "wherever you may be, do not let her die."

Now it is dusk. Quetit has had the smallpox for many nights and storm clouds gather in the sky. How much longer can a sickness last? The hut turns dark, like night. Thunder crashes and Woelfin throws tobacco on the fire to appease the angry spirits. Tummaa shivers and hides beneath my bed.

I wish I could be like a storm. Unleashing all my hurt in thunder. Bright sheets of lightning spark the air. Quetit awakens from a restless sleep.

"Little One. Do not be afraid. It is just a storm," I tell her, smoothing the hair away from her face.

"Tskinnak. I am not afraid," Quetit says, touching me, closing her fingers around my hand. She speaks more clearly than she has in days. "I had a dream. It was about the man of God. A robe of clouds covered him, white like snow." Quetit's voice fades, like the sound of a dying wind through corn.

"Tell me about the man of God," I say.

"The man of God sheltered us beneath his wings. He flew us to your home. Your home . . . it was bathed in sunlight." She shuts her eyes once more.

"Quetit. Who was standing in the door flap? Who was there to greet us?" I ask, wanting to hold her here with me; feel the warmth of a dream we have not shared in many moons.

"The sunlight hurt my eyes. I could not see. But I felt warm . . . like I do when you sing your mother's song. Sing it, Tskinnak, will you?"

I enfold Quetit in my arms. I feel her heart beat like my own. I want to fill her with my love. Give her the strength to live. I sing my mother's song for her. I sing it softly, over and over again, longing for the time when I was small and a mother sang this song to me.

The storm rages through the night. I hold Quetit and I sing until my throat turns raw. Like the slow unfurling

194

of a blossom, I begin to feel God's spirit move within me. And I realize then that He has always been there, like a small seed, buried in my heart.

Morning light awakens me. Morning light and Tummaa, poking his wet nose into my face. He is begging me to go outside. Quetit stirs in my arms.

She has survived the night. I don't know if it was the cool, clean air the storm brought or the singing of my mother's song. I hold my breath, afraid to dream of her recovery. The smallpox is fickle. Like the moon, it wanes and then it waxes.

But two days later, when Quetit sits up in bed and tells me she is tired of broth, that she wants deer meat for her breakfast, I know that she is better.

That morning, Tummaa and I greet the dawn together. With tears in my eyes, I ask God to forgive my anger and I thank Him for Quetit's life. She means everything to me. Tummaa barks. My tears turn to laughter when I see this old dog chase his tail, as if he were a puppy. He must feel the way I do, born anew.

What corn we have grows tall and ripens. There are not many of us left to gather it. Six women. Five children. Chief Towigh. The days grow short and I harvest walnuts. Soon cold will crack the trees and snow will fly once more. I dread its coming.

A chilly wind blows through the village the day the messenger arrives. A Tuscarora. His leggings are caked with mud. His face is gaunt.

"Brothers. I bring you this message with a heavy

heart," he says. "A white man's army mustered by the English marches through our land. It numbers as many warriors as there are stars in the winter sky. They carry guns, long knives that glitter. The white man's chief, a Swiss named Colonel Bouquet, says that we must bury our hatchets, return all prisoners taken in the war and pay for peace."

First the smallpox, now a white man's army. I feel the old cloak of despair cover me, feel a hard noose tighten around my neck. I don't know how we will survive this time.

At nightfall, Chief Towigh lights the council fire. "My people. Now this fire burns bright. But soon it will go out. Extinguished by our blood. I have seen our blood fill the streams until they overflow. The white man will not rest until he has destroyed the last of us. At sunrise, we must flee."

"The white man will hunt us wherever we place our blankets," Woelfin says. She stands beside Chief Towigh, holding herself erect with the oak limb she uses for a cane. "The Great Spirit has given us this land for a good purpose. Are we to abandon it like cowardly dogs? Hiding our tails between our legs and running for the nearest shelter?"

"Old woman. There are too few of us to fight." Chief Towigh's shoulders seem bowed by a burden too great to carry. My heart aches for him.

"Then flee," Woelfin says. "But I will remain. I will plant my soil and guard my hunting ground." She moves

196

stiffly around the council fire, poking at coals with her cane. I know that Woelfin has no choice but to remain. She is too weak, too old to travel.

"Old woman," Chief Towigh says. "If you stay here, you will die."

Hot embers fly from Woelfin's cane as she points it at Chief Towigh. "Hah! What does the white man want with me? One old woman with two daughters. One day you will return and you will find me here. I will be sucking marrow from a deer bone while my daughters grease my joints with oil."

"We have made our decision," Chief Towigh says. "I leave you with the freedom to make yours."

I say nothing to Woelfin about her choice. I know that it is madness. We cannot survive the winter on our own. But she stands so erect and proud, bold defiance, like firelight, giving life to her dark eyes. I will not take that life away. I respect her for it.

I mind Proud One's baby boy while she gathers her few belongings and packs them in a deerskin bag. He giggles when I tickle his belly, reminding me of Gokhas, Nonschetto's baby.

Somewhere in the land beyond our sight, Nonschetto must look down upon us now. Her face will sadden when she sees her people packing their belongings. I wish her spirit could descend, curl up inside my heart and tell me not to fear—that a white man's army with scalping knives and blazing guns will never cut and burn its way through our wooded hills and valleys.

At dawn, Flat Nose and I cover the ashes of our council fire. Red, orange and yellow, the leaves fall from our hands. Flat Nose weeps, a tall, ungainly woman who has lost her husband, lost her two sons, Stone Face and Running Water. I have never walked as a friend with Flat Nose, but now our eyes meet and we reach for each other. Like two lost souls, we wail as sunlight paints the sky the color of the falling leaves.

CHAPTER
Twenty-one

Frost covers the north wall of our hut and the morning air is damp and cold. I am Quetit's blanket. She shivers when I rise. "I will boil some broth to warm you." I wrap her in my ragged deerskin, wishing it were Woelfin's bearskin robe. Woelfin sleeps in shadows, burrowed in its warm dark folds. The outline of Woelfin's body looks small and frail beneath the bearskin. I have never noticed this before. It troubles me, but I don't know why.

Tummaa yawns and stretches. He shakes himself from nose to tail, then follows me outside. Our breath makes clouds in the freezing air.

No dogs howl. I hear no corn being ground in mortars. Four uneasy nights have passed since our people fled. The village feels as empty as the dusty bowls lined up beneath my bed. I shiver at the sound the wind makes as it blows through the naked trees, rattling their branches like old bones. Last night, a ghostly ring circled the moon, heralding a storm.

I run from hut to hut searching for scraps of food the others may have left. Flocks of hungry blackbirds screech as they ride the wind above me. I wonder what the blackbirds see.

The wind rises and the blackbirds alight in the locust trees behind Chief Towigh's hut. There, I gather fox and wildcat bones that I find scattered on the ground. The raven and the turkey buzzards have picked them clean. I hope Chief Towigh has escaped the white man's guns. I hope he's reached the promised land and that his fires burn bright. I wish I had a blackbird's wings so that I could ride the wind and see. Dark clouds are massing in the sky.

Tummaa rests his chin on his knees, watching me as I now feed the fire inside our hut and cook the bones in a pot of water. I add corn meal to the broth, but only a handful. We must ration what little corn we have. Winter is soon coming.

Woelfin stirs. Her bearskin hangs like bat's wings as she shuffles to the fire. I hand her a bowl of broth and her lips smack in appreciation as she tastes it.

I prepare another bowl for Quetit, wondering how we will survive the winter. Perhaps some people from another village will join us here and we can hunt together.

"You must gather walnuts before the storm breaks," Woelfin says, her head cocked as she listens to the wind.

"And kindling," I say, already beginning to feel burdened by these chores. Quetit is still weak from the smallpox. Chores are endless when you do them alone.

I turn to hand Quetit the bowl of broth and Tummaa begins to growl. I stare at him. His head is raised, his ears, pointed. He listens to some faraway sound I cannot hear.

Tummaa's hackles rise. He begins to walk toward the door flap.

"Tummaa. What is wrong?" I say, feeling my heartbeat quicken, for suddenly, I hear it, too. Something is moving outside our hut. It is not the tapping of a tree branch nor the wind blowing through the fallen leaves. It sounds like hoofbeats.

Woelfin grabs Tummaa. She wraps her hand around his mouth. "Be silent," she hisses.

The sudden quiet in our hut feels like the heavy calm before a storm. Quetit slips out of bed and runs to me. "Tskinnak," she whispers. "Who is coming here?"

I shake my head. I do not know. But I hear the sound of iron-shod hooves, the creak of leather. Steam rises from the pot, and I wish the telling scent of fox and wildcat bones would return to the broth.

"The white man," Woelfin whispers.

"No, it cannot be," I say, suddenly realizing that it could.

The sound of footsteps nears our hut and I don't know if I should rejoice or cry. Do guns await us or helpful arms? Last night I dreamt about the man of God.

"Lay down your weapons," a deep voice says. "Then come outside." The words are in the Indian tongue, but the tone is wrong. Not like an Indian's at all.

Woelfin holds a warning finger to her mouth, silencing Quetit and me. We huddle together, not knowing what to do.

The door flap slowly opens. A cold draft of air chills my neck and Quetit tightens her arms around me. Woelfin releases Tummaa and grabs a smoldering branch from the fire. Tummaa lunges at the door flap and I throw my arms around him, holding him back from the dark shape filling our door.

The long barrel of a rifle points toward me. "Tie the dog."

With trembling hands, I tether Tummaa to my bed with a rawhide strip. He braces his front feet on the packed earth floor and barks as I back away from him. I do not want to leave Tummaa, but the rifle barrel points at me, gesturing to come outside. A thousand drums begin to pound inside my head.

Quetit clings to me and we duck through the door flap. I feel the brush of bearskin as Woelfin follows close behind.

The man holding the rifle lowers it when he sees us. He has hair upon his face that is the color of the hills at sunset. He wears a large dark coat with shiny buttons. Behind him are more white men: some riding horses; some now creeping around our huts. All carry guns, long knives that glitter.

The men surround us with their weapons. Holding her smoldering branch before her as if it were a fiery shield, Woelfin shrieks, "You killed our people! Would you now scalp one old woman? Would you kill her daughters?"

Her cry cuts through me like a knife. Drum beats pound inside my head and I see our rivers red with blood. Above them, a dark cloud forms into a wolf's head, the totem of our clan.

"These are not your daughters," the white man says, his eyes searching mine, searching Quetit's. His eyes are strange. They are the color of a cloudless sky. He pushes up my sleeve and points to skin the sun has never darkened. I feel as if a storm were breaking. "What is your name?" he asks.

"Tskinnak," I whisper, wonder replacing my sense of fear. This man is taller than any Indian I have ever known and his skin is fair. Yet he speaks the Indian tongue. Is . . . he the man of God?

"And your name before Tskinnak? Your white man's name?"

"She was always Tskinnak. She is my daughter!" Woelfin tries to grab my arm and the white man pushes her away.

"No. Do not harm Woelfin," I say, placing myself between the two of them, feeling the sudden pull between a life I know and one I remember in my dreams. Is this the man of God?

"Where are you from?" the white man asks. His

voice is gentle and his eyes are kind, but I cannot answer him. How can one describe a dream?

Beside me, Quetit shivers.

"The child is not well." The man takes off his coat and helps me to dress Quetit in its warm dark folds. "The war is over," he tells us. "We have come to take you home."

Home?

Woelfin makes an awful sound. Like pottery when it cracks in fire. "This is Tskinnak's home!" She waves her branch at the empty huts. "Daughters! Tell the white man who you are. Tell him how Woelfin raised you. How you are flesh of her flesh, bone of her bone."

"Flesh of her flesh, bone of her bone," I whisper, feeling the anguish in these words. But how can I deny my dreams? "Woelfin raised me," I say softly, staring at the frozen ground. "She has shared her fire with me for many winters."

"She has held you prisoner many winters." The white man takes my hand. "Now you are free. Now you can go home."

Home.

"Tskinnak! Quetit!" Woelfin cries. "Tell the white man who you are!"

I feel as if I were being torn in two. How many winters have I waited for the man of God? How many winters have I shared Woelfin's fire? Who *am* I?

The sky above is dark with clouds and seems to hold no answers. The white man leads Quetit and me to a chestnut horse. I have seen a horse like this before. Was it in my dream? I remember . . . a wagon, an oak tree and an awful smell, like burning flesh. Quetit sobs and pulls on my arm. "Tskinnak. If we go with the white man, Woelfin will be all alone and she will die."

It is then I recall how Woelfin looked when she was sleeping, small and frail. I cannot leave her; make her face the coming winter on her own. She . . . *is* a part of me.

Tummaa barks. "Tskinnak!" Woelfin screams.

I turn around. Flames are rising from our hut. A thin, dark man carries a lighted torch. He runs from one hut to the next, setting each on fire.

"No!" I scream at the white man. "Stop him! He is burning down my home!"

The white man grips my arm. His fingers are like iron. "It is war," he says.

"You said the war was over!" I wrench myself out of his hold. Sobs choke me as I race across the clearing. Tummaa is tied to my bed! Tummaa will burn!

Flames lick at the door flap as I stumble through. Tummaa cowers beneath my bed. How could I leave my dog? What is wrong with me? I struggle to untie him.

Woelfin grabs the hunting knife she keeps in her basket. She cuts Tummaa's tether, then takes the rawhide leash. Flames singe me as I follow her outside.

"Woelfin?" I choke upon her name as she brushes me aside.

"Go, you ungrateful child! Go with the white man,"

she says. Tummaa struggles against his leash as he tries to reach me. Woelfin pulls him back, drags him with her around the bonfire circle and away from me.

Dear God, my dreams have deceived me into betraying those I love. Frantic, I run after Woelfin, wanting to make amends, wanting to tell her, "I will never leave you. You *are* my flesh, my bone." The bearded white man shouts. Two soldiers in red coats grab my arms. They drag me back to the chestnut horse, to Quetit, who struggles in a white man's arms. What is happening to us? Is this what dreams can bring?

My heart aches as, held back by the white man, I see Woelfin's small dark shape hurry past Flat Nose's hut and disappear into the forest. Will she and Tummaa find shelter there? A hollow log? Will an angel bring them food? "Woelfin!" I hear myself wail.

Quetit, sobbing, throws herself into my arms. We support each other while all around us the soldiers shout in a strange tongue we cannot understand. They fire their rifles into the sky. Flames, like bloodied rags, rise from Chief Towigh's hut.

"Tskinnak. What has happened to the man of God?" Quetit whispers the question, but it seems to echo through the sky.

And now, the rain begins.

206

CHAPTER
Twenty-two

Quetit and I ride the white man's horse. The path that we are riding down is narrow. Wet branches brush against our naked legs, against our horse's flanks. The rain has stopped, but the sky is still dark with clouds.

We travel to the white man's camp and from there we will be taken to a fort. Messengers will be sent across the land to tell our families that we are alive and free. Then our families will take us home. The bearded white man told me this in the Indian tongue. For when he spoke to me as if I were a white man, I could not understand at all.

Quetit rests her head against my chest. The smell of smoke still clings to Quetit's hair. She is crying. She has been crying ever since we left our village. My arms ache from holding her.

I do not know who I am. When I search my memory for the glimmer of a white man's name, all I hear is Woelfin's cry, telling me I am Tskinnak, flesh of Woelfin's flesh, bone of her bone.

I do not know from where I came. Do I still have a home? Does anyone wait there for me? I try to recall the warm house I envisioned in my dreams, but all I see is our burning hut and Woelfin, being swallowed by the trees.

The bearded white man walks on one side of our horse. His hand holds the bridle. The dark man who set the fire walks on the other side. He cradles his musket in his arms. All white men seem to carry muskets. Will they greet us with them when we reach the white man's camp? I am afraid of going there. I have lived nine winters with the Indians, and I don't know who I am.

We pass the village of the Tuscaroras. I smell no wood smoke. No dogs howl. Huts stand like empty turtle shells. A white willow's branches arch above the path. I hear them whisper as we pass and I wonder, who will gather the willow bark when Woelfin's joints ache with cold? Who will brew her tea? Will she greet the dawn with Tummaa? Oh, dear Lord, I miss them. I wish this day had never dawned.

The cries of geese echo through the sky—a lonely, aching sound. The bearded white man lifts his hand and halts the line of soldiers following behind. The soldiers talk together. They all talk at once. I don't know how they can understand what anyone says. They should be like the Indian, who listens politely as each man speaks.

Quetit starts to cough. Her cough is deep and loud. "She barks like a dog." The dark man speaks in the

Indian tongue, but his eyes are a white man's eyes, pale and staring. "Make her stop crying."

"Quetit has had the smallpox. She is too weak to handle sorrow." I make myself speak the Indian words slowly, so that he will understand.

He brings out a flask. He takes a long drink, wipes his mouth and hands the flask to me. "Give her some of this." He nods his head at Quetit.

The flask smells of white man's whiskey. Tiger Claw was drunk on whiskey the day he mistook Namoes for a white man. He bit off Namoes's ear. I tell the dark man, "No."

He waves his musket at the woods. "Do you want the savages to hear her?"

"Our people are not savages! They will not harm us."

"They will. You ride with the white man now."

His words sting me like a thousand bees.

"Give her the whiskey," the bearded white man says.

"Will the whiskey stop her crying?"

"It will make her sleep."

I look into Quetit's eyes. They are full of pain and sorrow. I give her the whiskey. She cries each time after it goes down. "The whiskey burns." She buries her head into the hollow of my shoulder.

I hear the rain before I feel it. The sound of raindrops on leaves. The bearded white man shouts his orders. We move on. A pack of soldiers breaks off from our line.

The dark man leads them through a laurel thicket and then they are gone.

Quetit coughs and shakes with cold. I wrap myself around her and sing my mother's song, thinking of the day Nonschetto died. This song was our comfort then. It is our only comfort now. Slowly, sleep steals over Quetit. I feel her soft breath warm my neck.

The rhythm of the horse's walk, the sound of raindrops, lull me. I dream of Quetit. She is strong, as she was before the smallpox. She dances in the firelight at Proud One's wedding feast while Woelfin watches from the shadows. I can almost feel Tummaa nuzzling my hand, smell the burning hickory.

And then the burning hickory becomes a raging fire and I see Woelfin burning in the flames. I feel my way through thick, dark smoke, trying to reach her, but I never do. And then, Tummaa begins to bark.

A horse's whinney startles me and I awaken feeling bereft. Our horse is prancing up a small incline while the bearded soldier struggles to hold him back. The woods are thinner now. We crest the hill and I hear a droning sound, like bees gathered at a hive.

A valley spreads out below us, bounded by the broad Muskingum River. Horses, cows, sheep and oxen graze on the rich meadowland. Rough-hewn huts, tents made of some strange white animal skin, palisade fences and wagons dot the wooded slopes beyond. I smell the smoke of many fires, and I am afraid.

We have reached the white man's camp.

The droning sound grows louder and our horse plunges down the hill. The ground dips and through the rain, I now see a band of soldiers marching through a muddy field. They carry rifles with long knives jutting out from the barrel tips.

The bearded white man stops our horse and aims his rifle at the sky. He fires three shots. All around us, the soldiers begin to shout.

"Tskinnak!" Quetit's hands clutch at me.

"Shhhh. It is only the soldiers announcing our arrival." I rest my cheek against her hair that smells of smoke and bear grease. Beneath my hands I feel Quetit's heart beat, quick and sudden, like a captive bird's.

A flock of sheep scatters as three dark horses gallop toward us through the muddy bottom of the meadowland. Soldiers wearing bright red coats, leggings made from golden cloth, and high black boots spur the horses on.

The hoofbeats seem to pound inside my head. I look down at Quetit, wearing her torn deerskin sacque. I hear the soldiers rein the horses to a dead standstill. For a moment, there is silence. I stare at my broad dark hands, afraid to meet the blueness in the soldiers' eyes. Afraid to marvel at the paleness in their skins. For in this heavy silence I see with a soldier's eyes—a girl, almost eleven winters old; a young woman, twenty. Both of them, more Indian than white.

CHAPTER
Twenty-three

There are more white men here than there are stars in the winter sky. After six nights of living in their camp, I have grown accustomed to the sight of them. Some wear coats the color of the setting sun. Some wear fringed deerskin and fine moccasins, thicker and sturdier than mine. Others wear the dark, somber clothing that now covers me.

The soldiers carry rifles, but they also keep thread and needles in their deerskin bags and, I have discovered, compassion in their hearts. Two fair-skinned soldiers took the coats off their backs to make this sacque for me. Laughing, they corralled two other soldiers and took their coats to make a sacque for Quetit too.

Quetit and I watched these soldiers cut and sew. Quetit's eyes were like a startled owl's. Men doing women's work is like snow when honeybees swarm.

These clothes keep my body warm, but my hands are cold. I warm them over a fire which burns inside the long house the soldiers built to shelter us. Four fires burn within this house. They cast strange shadows. Snakelike arms move through the smokey air. Bodies appear as dark hump-backed shapes.

Women and children form the shadows. Like Quetit and me, they were captured by the Indians. Most of them look and talk like we do. Warriors have brought them to this white man's camp. They have returned them to the white man in return for peace.

When I first entered this camp, I felt like a rabbit caught in a trap. But Mrs. Post, the white woman who now cares for us, took me in hand and freed me from my fear. She is kind. She feeds us stew thick with meat and corn. She bakes bread that is soft and filling. When Quetit awakens, cold and shaking from a nightmare, Mrs. Post will cluck and fuss, as if Quetit were her chick.

Mrs. Post treats us as if we were her daughters. Many winters ago, her only child was captured by Indians. Mrs. Post has been searching for her ever since. White Flower told me this, for she speaks and understands the white man's tongue. White Flower said that Mrs. Post's child has a mark on her cheek that is the size and color of a wild strawberry. Has anyone seen her?

No one has.

White Flower now sleeps on the platform bed in back of me. For three long winters, she lived with the Shawnee. White Flower said that she was traded from

213

one family to another and knew the fires of many homes. Warriors brought her to this white man's camp four nights ago.

White Flower has a birthmark on her arm that is shaped like a locust leaf. When Indians brought her to this camp, I saw a soldier kiss this birthmark. He lifted White Flower and swung her through the air. He called her "daughter." He said that, once the army is disbanded, he will take her home. But for now, White Flower must stay with the other women and children. She will be safe and cared for there.

I wish a father would find me at this camp. I wish he would take me in his arms and swing me through the air.

Colonel Bouquet, the white man's chief, has eyes like White Flower's father. His eyes are dark and kind, and they miss nothing. He speaks some Indian. He asked me my white name.

I could not answer him.

He asked me where I came from.

I could not say.

"Do you remember anything about your family? Your father? Your mother?" he asked me.

I told him, "No."

Colonel Bouquet placed his hand upon my cheek. "Something will happen. Something will come to you. Then you will remember."

For one moment, I laid my cheek against his hand. Then he was gone.

I did not tell him of the dream I have. A dream I do not even share with Quetit. In my dream, a mother now holds me in her arms the way that White Flower's father held her. My mother smells like Mrs. Post, of wood smoke and baking bread. My mother's hair shines in the firelight. Her hair is the color of the hickory nut once its rind is peeled. My mother's skin is like white willow leaves, soft and silky.

I know this dream is wishful thinking. And I know the horrors that believing in a dream can bring. But it haunts me, as does Woelfin. I don't know what has happened to her. I pray she has found shelter from the winter wind. So many spirits haunt my sleep.

A shadow now moves across my face. White Flower begins to scream. She thrashes on the bed in back of me. White Flower's hands are like a bird's wings. They flutter across the many scars which mark her face.

I try to take these hands in mine.

"Do not touch me!" White Flower screams.

"It is just me. Tskinnak. You have been dreaming," I say. I know the anguish of her dreams like I know my own. At night we have shared our memories. White Flower and I are kindred spirits. I feel as if I've known her for a long, long time.

White Flower's eyes are dark and wild. She pulls away from me. She stands and quickly walks outside. Quetit looks up anxiously from the lump of bread dough Mrs. Post has given her to keep her small hands busy. "It's all right," I tell her. "Everything will be all right." The sounds of whispers trail me as I follow after White Flower.

The tattered robe she wears flutters in the wind like broken feathers. I see her seek the shelter of a tree that grows beside the river. She sits down, nestled by its roots.

I follow and sit beside her, and I wait.

"I am sorry. Did I frighten you?" White Flower finally says.

"Not as much as your dreams frighten you."

"An eagle held me in his talons." White Flower points to the scars which mark her face. She does not touch them. "Suddenly, he let me go. Tskinnak, I am afraid."

"It is only a dream."

"When I lived with eagles, I learned the eagles' way. I cooked horse liver in a caul of bear fat to please my masters. I repaired torn clothing for scraps of food. My tongue learned to remain silent, so that blows would not rain upon my head. Now I am falling. I do not know where I will land."

"Your father is here. Once the peace talks are over, he will take you home," I say, thinking of a burning hut, a dream.

A smile, like sunlight through this wind-blown tree, crosses White Flower's face. She sighs, hugs her legs and rests her chin upon her knees, her long black hair curtaining her face. Upstream, a sentinel halloos, telling us that all is well. But the wind off the river brings the sad wailing of two Indian women mourning the loss of the adopted white children they've turned over to a soldier's arms. This camp is no-man's-land.

White Flower shudders. I lean my cheek against her shoulder, wanting to let her know that I am here. That I understand the way she feels.

We sit together, she and I. We watch the sunlight dance on water.

Where does the river flow?

CHAPTER
Twenty-four

I have cut my hair. I have braided the dark strands together to make a bracelet for White Flower.

"I will wear it always," she tells me. "It will remind me of you."

White Flower now rides behind her father on a large bay horse. She waves good-bye and I see this bracelet; a dark band against dark skin. White Flower is going home.

Quetit sleeps beside me in this wagon piled with bags of corn. We have been traveling for many days through woods and boggy bottomland. Sometimes we walk. Sometimes the soldiers allow us to ride in the wagon— those times when our legs are weary and our feet, blistered. Now we are but one day's ride from the white man's council house, the one he calls Fort Pitt.

Quetit has grown stronger on the white man's food. But sadness continues to haunt her, as it does me. Each morning I awaken hoping to feel Tummaa's cold nose nuzzling my face. I miss my large gray dog. I miss Woelfin, all the villagers I had grown to love.

218

White Flower's horse is just a bright spot in the trees. Now it, too, is gone.

I try to look ahead of me. But cattle, sheep, pack horses, soldiers and this endless forest block my view. A soldier cracks his whip and a stray cow lumbers ahead of him, then veers off to join the herd. I can count the bones beneath her hide. I don't think she'll survive this journey.

Captives freed by the white man walk beside our wagon. Some walk behind. They form a ragged line, hushed now, save for the occasional crying of a child. Many wear clothes the soldiers made. A few are still dressed like Indians. The air smells of dead leaves and horses.

There are over two hundred of us being taken to Fort Pitt. White Flower's father was the one who counted us, who wrote down our names—Experience Wood, John Ice, Molly Mitch, Joseph Red Jacket, Quetit, Tskinnak . . . One by one he asked us: "How many shirts do you own? Did the Indians give you leggings? Shoe packs? Blankets?" He drew marks upon a paper as we answered him. I do not know why.

A woman shares this wagon with us now. Her head is bowed. She hides her head between her shoulders as a turtle hides within its shell. She was captured by the Delawares and shared their fires for many winters. A Delaware Chief is her husband. They have a son about eight winters old who rides a horse that is tethered to this wagon. The boy's hands are tied. His feet are hobbled. If the white man did not hobble him, he would run away.

"How can I enter my parents' dwelling?" this woman

suddenly says, looking upward to the sky, as if the gray clouds held an answer. Her face is pinched and lined with worry. Her searching eyes alight on me. "I am married to an Indian Chief," she says. "I bring home a son who hates the white man. Will my parents understand? Will they be kind to him? And my old companions. Will they associate with me?"

"I do not know," I whisper.

She stares at the talisman she holds tightly in her hands—a small pipe with the bowl carved into the shape of a wolf's head, the totem of her husband's clan. She says no more.

Her silence troubles me as much as her anguished questions do. I bow my head and close my eyes. I listen to the creak of wagon wheels and try to sleep.

At night we camp beneath the stars. Soldiers talk as they stand guard. Wolves and owls make a great noise in the night. The horses are restless.

I wake early in the morning. The woman's son, sullen-faced and silent, sits tethered between two soldiers. His mother is gone.

The soldiers search, but they do not find her. I wish her a safe journey to her husband's side, but I feel empty when I see her son, bound and shackled as he rides the horse still tethered to the wagon. I know how he must feel—abandoned, with nothing to look forward to.

We slowly follow the course of the Ohio River. Quetit, nestled beside me in the wagon, holds up a loop of rawhide thread. "Tskinnak? Will you play with me?"

I place my hands inside the loop. I finger-weave a shape out of the thread. I feel the boy's eyes on me as Quetit slips this shape onto her hands. Her fingers fly as she weaves the outline of a cradle. I take the cradle and weave a ladder out of it. Back and forth we play the weaving game, until my fingers slip.

Quetit lays the empty loop upon her lap. She rests her head against my shoulder. "Tskinnak," she says. "What is going to happen to us?"

I sigh, swallowing my impatience. Quetit has asked this question many times. I put my arm around her. "We will stay at Fort Pitt until the soldiers are disbanded."

"And then?"

"Colonel Bouquet will try to find our families."

"Tskinnak." Quetit's eyes look into mine. "I don't remember anything about my white man's family."

"I know."

"But you remember yours. You've told me about your mother. You said her arms were warm." Quetit burrows herself between my arms, as if her warmth could bring back my memories. "You said your mother told stories and sang lullabies to you. How will we know this mother when we see her?"

"Little one. My mother may not be alive."

"But if she is, how will we know her? What does she look like?"

Quetit knows the answer to this question too, for I have answered it before. All I recall of my mother is a dark mist and a wagon pulled by two strong oxen. But now, the burden of an endless journey overwhelms me.

"I have a dream," I tell Quetit.

"Yes?" she says.

"In my dream, my mother's hair is the color of the hickory nut once its rind is peeled and her hands are like white willow leaves, pale and silky." As I give voice to these words, they take on a reality I have never felt before. They *must* be true.

Quetit raises her head and smiles at me. "Does your mother have eyes like yours or mine?"

"Her eyes are green, like moss."

"Does your mother have a long nose or a short one?" Quetit giggles.

I squeeze her gently. "Quetit. Your questions make my head ache."

"Tskinnak. Can we pray that this mother will find us?"

"We can pray." I search the sky. Somewhere above the clouds God listens to our prayers. God understands why we have to believe in dreams. He understands what I no longer want to say to myself or Quetit—

That the one clear memory that haunts me most is a scalp that used to hang inside our hut.

My father's scalp.

CHAPTER
Twenty-five

We follow the Ohio to where it meets the river the soldiers call the Allegheny. Across the Allegheny stands Fort Pitt. Like hills, its great walls rise above the water.

The soldiers "halloo" at the fort. They load their muskets and fire them at the sky.

From the far side of the Allegheny comes an answering "halloo." Then a loud noise sounds, like the roar of an angry bear. Smoke fills the sky above Fort Pitt. Another roar and then another sounds.

"Tskinnak. These big guns frighten me. Why must the soldiers make such noise?" Quetit says, covering her ears.

"It is the white man's way," I say, longing for the sound of a single Indian halloo. The white man's welcome makes my head ache.

Now a boat moves swiftly down the river. Two soldiers pole the craft toward the wooded bank where we are waiting. A large man dressed in deerskin wades into the water. He pulls the boat to shore.

The two soldiers talk to Colonel Bouquet. Colonel

Bouquet gives his orders. We will make camp on the banks of the Allegheny. Tomorrow, many boats and rafts will come. They will take us to the fort.

The sun sets before our fires are lit. Quetit and I eat our supper cold. It is bread, dried beef and water.

Peg, the large dark woman the soldiers call "the mulatto," crouches near us while we eat. She patiently roasts fresh venison over a fire that she has kindled. Her husband, a tall and handsome Mingo Indian, waits for her in the shadows just beyond our camp.

This Mingo has walked with Peg on the long journey to Fort Pitt. Each night, he has brought her fresh venison to eat. The soldiers have allowed him to bring her food. But they have warned the Mingo not to follow Peg when she is taken to her home in the land they call Virginia. The Mingo will be in danger there. Peg's family will shoot him.

"I would live in her sight or die in her presence," I heard the Mingo reply, "for what pleasure shall the Mingo have if Peg is gone? Who will cook his venison? Who will thank him for soft fur?"

The venison is cooked. Peg carries the wooden spit that holds the hot and dripping meat over to her husband. I hear the soft murmur of their talk as they eat together. Quetit and I both hope the Mingo stays with Peg. They fit together like a well-made bow and arrow.

Clouds cover the moon. Soldiers crouch by fires and clean their muskets. They polish their long knives until they shine. Quetit and I bed down beneath the trees. We share one blanket, and we pray.

Early in the morning, the soldiers come with boats and rafts, and we cross the swiftly flowing river. The cold spray of water stings my cheeks.

We climb a steep and muddy bank and wait for the others who have yet to cross. Quetit's skin is the color of ashes. I rub her arms to warm her.

Once everyone is safe on shore, the soldiers line us up. They flank us on all sides. They march beside us down the path that leads around the fort.

A large ditch that is filled with water stops our march. Like the great walls that rise like hills, this ditch surrounds Fort Pitt. A soldier shouts and a gate is lowered to form a bridge.

I hold Quetit's hand. Soldiers march on either side as we cross the bridge and walk the long dark passage which leads through the walls and into the fort. We enter a wide, flat plain surrounded by stone walls. Bands of soldiers march upon the plain. They carry sticks holding brightly colored cloths. They beat on drums and blow on pipes that make a wailing sound.

I bow my head and watch my feet. I place one foot before the other. Mud cakes my moccasins. All around me I hear the soldiers march, their voices raised in triumph.

Drumbeats mark our days. Drumbeats and the sounds of marching. But soon the beat of drums will cease and the soldiers will disband.

One band of soldiers has already left Fort Pitt. They march to Virginia. They take some captives with them. Peg is gone. I hope the Mingo follows her. I heard that Colonel Bouquet talked to him. That he gave the Mingo a handsome present to make him stay behind. Mary was the one who told me. She is a thin woman with a long and hungry face. "The Mingo is a heathen," Mary said. "Peg is better off without him."

Quetit and I think that Mary is a silly goose. No one is better suited to Peg than the Mingo. I pray they are together now.

I sit on my narrow bed in the long gray house the soldiers call the barracks. Quetit squats on the floor in front of me while I comb lice from her hair. I want to make Quetit pretty for when she goes to Carlisle. The soldiers are to take us there. We leave tomorrow.

They will take more than one hundred of us to this white man's town. It is a ten days' march from here. Colonel Bouquet has already sent messengers ahead. They post signs all through the white man's land. The signs say that those who lost friends and family in the war are to come to Carlisle and that we will meet them there.

I will be glad to leave Fort Pitt. The soldiers have crammed us into these dark barracks like minnows in a net. We have nothing to do here and so we talk. At times our talk is friendly. At times our talk grows loud and angry.

Today a soldier named Matthew brought us leggings.

There were not enough for each of us to have a pair and so we fought over them.

Sour Plums, a large fat woman who lived with the Seneca, brought out colored stones from her deerskin pouch. "We will throw dice for the leggings," she said, separating the women into groups.

I wear my leggings now. They are unlike any I have ever worn. They are thick and rough. They itch like straw. But they cover the scars that mark my legs and feet and they are new.

The soldier Matthew said the leggings are called "stockings." I will wear my "stockings" when I go to Carlisle.

Sour Plums is snoring. She sleeps by herself in a bed that is next to the one I share with Quetit. Sour Plums wears three necklaces. They are made of brightly colored beads.

I wish that I could have a necklace, too.

Through the barrack's door, I see the flat ground where the soldiers march. Snow now falls upon the ground. The flakes are like white flowers.

If I could, I would bead the flakes. I would make a necklace out of them.

In my mind, I wear the necklace now and I am in Carlisle. I walk toward a woman. Her hair is the color of the hickory nut. Her skin is pale. She holds out her arms to me.

In my new stockings and my necklace, I am as beautiful as snow.

CHAPTER
Twenty-six

It is dusk. A light snow falls and three men dressed in hunting frocks greet us with their lanterns as we enter Carlisle. Colonel Bouquet talks to these men and I stare at the log buildings, the large fort that forms one side of the center square. I do not remember this white man's town. I don't think I've ever been here.

Now Colonel Bouquet speaks to us all. He says the soldiers will divide us up in groups. Some of us will be sheltered in the fort. Others will share the white man's homes. In the morning, we will meet together in this square. Our families come tomorrow.

I grip Quetit's hand as one of the men in the hunting frocks leads us down a snow-covered path. His hands are large and gentle as he ushers us into a home that smells of baking bread. The white man's wife greets us at the door. She is short and plump. Three small children hide behind her skirts.

"Tskinnak. Look! They have a dog like Tummaa!" Quetit points to a big gray dog who now bounds through the open door. He shakes himself from nose to tail, spraying all of us with snow. I offer him my outstretched hands.

The white man's wife touches me. She points to the dog who offers me his paw. "Matchlock," she says.

"Matchlock." I repeat the dog's name as I accept his welcome.

The woman points to herself. "Anna."

"Anna," Quetit says, smiling shyly at the woman.

The children giggle as their mother names them all for us: Hans, Gerta and Peter. The father she calls Jacob.

The children have trouble saying my name and Quetit's. But they soon come out from behind their mother's skirts to play the weaving game with us. I am surprised that they know how.

We sit down to a supper of bread, cheese, milk and dried apples. Jacob bows his head before we eat. I know what he is doing.

Jacob is giving thanks.

While we are eating, I notice a large wooden box attached to the cabin wall—just above a large chest with a blanket folded on it. I . . . remember a box like this. My family had one. Something precious was stored inside it.

The box draws me like a bee to pollen. I sign to Anna, "May I open it?"

Anna smiles and nods her head.

I take a heavy book out of the box and place it on the table. Everyone is watching me.

"What is it?" Quetit asks as I turn the fragile pages.

"It . . . it is the book of God," I say.

Anna asks me a question. I can tell by her tone, the look in her eyes. I sign to her, "I do not understand."

Anna points to the book.

My eyes become riveted on the words printed on the open page. For these words speak to me:

> The Lord sets the prisoners free;
> the Lord opens the eyes of the blind.
> The Lord lifts up those who are bowed down. . . .

I close the book. Afraid to look at it.

"Tskinnak. What is wrong? Your face is pale," Quetit says.

"Quetit. This must be a dream. I cannot understand the white man's tongue. And yet . . . I can read the words printed in this book as if they were my own."

"That is because they are not the white man's words. They are the words of God." Quetit's voice echoes the awe I feel. The man of God we waited for never came. But the word of God . . . it lives. It breathes within the pages of this book. In me.

"Tskinnak," Quetit says. "Read the words aloud."

And so I open the book once more to a page that has been well worn with use. "The Lord is my . . ." I cannot read the next word.

"Shepherd," Anna says without even looking at the page. She is smiling.

"The Lord is my shepherd, I shall not want." I continue to read the words that follow, and suddenly I feel as if I've come full circle, back to my beginnings, for this is the psalm my father often read to me. I remember now and remembering, I read:

Surely goodness and mercy shall follow me
All the days of my life;
And I shall dwell in the house of the Lord forever.

I can read no more, for now I think of Nonschetto's goodness, Woelfin's sense of pride and . . . compassion. I think of a clearing where I prayed to God and kept his words within my heart like stitches quilled in deerskin. And I remember a tree stump growing new branches by a stream. I hug the book to my chest, feeling Jacob's eyes upon me, as he holds little Gerta in his arms.

At night, Quetit and I gaze out the window in the sleeping loft we share. The snow has ended and the sky is clear. The sky seems endless, the stars so bright.

"Tskinnak. Remember the story of the woman falling through the sky?" Quetit says, resting her head against my shoulder.

"I remember."

"She fell through a night like this toward a land she had never seen. Was she afraid?"

"Perhaps. But birds held her aloft. They softened her fall."

Starlight now touches Quetit's face, setting it aglow. She sighs. "I believe the word of God is like a bird."

Morning comes, bringing the sound of wagon wheels, of soldiers' knocking on the cabin door. It is time to leave this kind shelter.

Anna hugs me and I cling to her. Little Gerta cries. Outside, the sky is once more overcast with clouds. The soldiers lead us to the village square. Now they line us up with all the other captives.

I see mountains in the distance, capped by snow and clouds and I think of Woelfin and Tummaa, lost somewhere beyond them. People are crying. Crowds of people push past the soldiers who are there to hold them back. I do not recognize any of the faces that I can see, but I know the anguish and the hope reflected in each one of them.

A thin, dark woman, bent like a reed in wind, rushes past. She speaks with a soldier. Her hands flutter as she points to one captive child, then to another. The soldier sadly shakes his head. The woman begins to cry. A tall man, scarred by smallpox, stares at Quetit, then at me.

"Do you know him?" Quetit whispers.

"No," I answer, disturbed by the pock marks on his face. They remind me of Tiger Claw, of Clear Sky and Gokhotit. They all are gone.

A woman with hair the color of snow touches my arm. I feel the anguish in her voice as she now questions me. I find I cannot look at her. Nothing I could do or say would be of any comfort. I wish I had the book of God right now. I wish that I could hold it, feel its reassurance. The Lord opens the eyes of the blind. He sets the prisoners free.

"Tskinnak!" Quetit points out a woman who hurries through the crowds. She wears a long, gray dress and her face is all sharp angles. It is her hair that fixes me.

Her hair is the color of the hickory nut.

I grab Quetit's hand and pull her through the milling people, keeping my eyes on the woman. Wanting to feel her eyes on mine.

Like the snowflakes that slowly drift down from the sky, this woman moves toward me.

Mother?

The woman looks beyond me. She cries out a white man's name as she runs toward a small, red-haired boy dressed in ragged deerskin. And in that instant, I know a dream has died.

"Tskinnak. Do not cry." Quetit wraps her arms around me and we watch the woman. Now she boards her wagon. She holds her little boy as if she will never let him go.

The waiting minutes feel like hours. The crowds get thinner now. Quetit is crying and I feel as if my heart will break. The white man does not adopt his captives. Not like the Indian. Where will *we* go? Will Jacob and Anna offer us their shelter? For how long?

"Tskinnak." Colonel Bouquet is calling my name. The woman with the hair like snow stands beside him, looking small, like a wren covered with soft flakes of snow.

"This woman thinks she knows you," he says as Quetit and I approach.

The woman brushes the hair from my face. I force myself to look at her, recognize the pain, the loss that must burn inside her as it burns in me.

"Many winters ago, Indians took her daughter prisoner," Colonel Bouquet says. "She resembled you. But the woman's memory is of a child, not of a grown girl, tall and dark."

The woman's eyes search mine. If I could part the mists that shroud my memory and see her standing in my door flap, my heart would sing. This woman's face is kind.

"I do not know her," I tell the Colonel, wishing that I did.

"Do you remember anything about your mother? Anything at all?" he says.

"No . . . just that my mother sang to me," I say. "And she told me stories from the great book in which God speaks to man."

Colonel Bouquet turns to the woman. Does he tell her what I say? The woman is crying. A young man dressed in deerskin hurries over to comfort her.

Beside me, Quetit shivers. I lift her face so that her eyes meet mine. "Little one. Remember last night, what you said about the word of God?"

"I remember."

"God's wings will give us shelter and His wings are strong. They will shelter this woman, too." I feel the comfort of these words even as I say them.

I gaze at the woman now. She stands between the young man and the Colonel, but she still looks at me. The snow is falling and her shawl is frayed. She must be cold. How far has she traveled?

Behind her, in the distance, I see mountains shrouded

by the snow. Then in the wind, I hear a trembling voice now sing:

> Alone, yet not alone am I,
> Though in this solitude so drear.

When Quetit had the smallpox, I sang this song for her. And now, the woman with the hair like snow sings this song for me.

My mother's song.

My throat tightens with wonder. Could this woman be my mother? Tears sting my eyes, but I sing too:

> I feel my Savior always nigh,
> He comes the weary hours to cheer,

And as I sing:

> I am with Him and He with me,
> Even here alone I cannot be.

I feel a mother's arms enfold me.

"Regina," she whispers.

"Regina." I repeat the name and it seems to echo through me. "I . . . am . . . Regina."

Quetit's sweet high voice breaks through the echo of my name. She sings my mother's song while all around her the snow is falling. I take her hand, drawing her into a warmth that for nine long winters I have only felt in dreams.

I want to grab the wonder of this moment and freeze it like a leaf in ice. My mother holds us now and my heart beats with joy. I give thanks for things that time nor circumstance can ever change—a mother's love, a song. . . .

Afterword

Regina Leininger was reunited with her mother on December 31, 1764. The young man dressed in deerskin was Regina's brother, John. Regina and Quetit went home with them to live in a snug cabin set in the Tulpehockan area of Pennsylvania. Perhaps Regina's sister, Barbara, joined them there. Both she and Marie LeRoy escaped from the Indians after three and one-half years of captivity.

In February, Regina and her mother walked seventy miles to visit with Henry Melchior Muhlenberg, a prominent Lutheran minister who lived outside of Philadelphia.

Regina asked him if she could have a copy of the book in which God speaks to man.

The Reverend Muhlenberg gave her a Bible. And he watched in wonder as Regina, who spoke only Indian in everyday matters, read whole passages of the Bible aloud in German.

He recorded the moving story of her captivity in his pastoral reports.

With Bible in hand, Regina returned to the home she loved. There she lived her life encircled by the warmth of family. Regina never married.

Now, more than two centuries later, a tombstone stands in Christ's Church cemetery near present-day Stouchsburg, Pennsylvania. The inscription on it reads:

Regina Leininger
In Legend Regina Hartman
As a small child held Indian captive
1755-1763
Identified by her mother's singing the hymn:
"Allein, Und Doch Nicht Ganz Allein."*

*"Alone, Yet Not Alone Am I."

Author's note: There was a change in the English calendar during this time which accounts for the discrepancy in years. The date on the tombstone should read "1764."

Selected Bibliography

Axtell, James. "The White Indians of Colonial America." *William and Mary Quarterly* 32 (January 1975): 55–88.

Bouquet's Expedition Against the Indians in 1764. Ohio Valley Historical Series. Cincinnati: Rober Clarke Co., 1907.

Brinton, Daniel G., and Anthony, Rev. Albert Sequaqkind, eds. *A Lenape—English Dictionary.* Philadelphia: Historical Society of Pennsylvania, 1888.

Brown, Honorable Isaac B. *Historical Sketches of Carlisle.* Harrisburg: William Stanley Ray, State Printer, 1905.

Dahlinger, Charles. "Fort Pitt." *Western Pennsylvania History Magazine* 5, no. 1:1–44.

Drake, Samuel. *Indian Captivities or Life in the Wigwam.* Auburn: Derby & Miller, 1851.

Ewing, William S. "Indian Captives Released by Colonel Bouquet," *Western Pennsylvania History Magazine* 39:187–203.

Hazard, Samuel, ed. *The Register of Pennsylvania,* vol. IV, pp. 390–391. Philadelphia: Wm. F. Geddes, Printer, 1829.

Heckewelder, John. *History, Manners, and Customs of the Indian Nations Who Once Inhabited Pennsylvania and the Neighboring States.* Reprinted from a copy in the State Historical Society of Wisconsin Library: Arno Press and the New York Times, 1971.

Horowitz, David. *The First Frontier: The Indian Wars and America's Origins: 1606–1776.* New York: Simon & Schuster, 1978.

Hunter, William A. *Forts on the Pennsylvania Frontier.* Harrisburg: Pennsylvania Historic and Museum Commission, 1960.

Jenkins, Howard M. *Pennsylvania Colonial and Federal 1608–1903,* vol. I. Philadelphia: Pennsylvania Historical Publications Association, 1903.

LeRoy, Marie, and Leininger, Barbara. "Narrative of Marie LeRoy and Barbara Leininger." In *Pennsylvania Archives,* series II, vol. 7, pp. 428–438. Harrisburg: Edwin K. Meyers, printer, 1891.

Mittelberger, Gottlieb. *Gottlieb Mittelberger's Journey to Pennsylvania in the Year 1750 and Return to Germany in the Year 1754.* Translated by Carl Theodore Eben. Philadelphia: John Jos McVey, 1888.

Muhlenberg, Henry Melchior. *The Journals of Henry Melchior Muhlenberg,* vol. II. Translated by Theodore G. Tappert and John W. Doberstein. Philadelphia: The Evangelical Lutheran Ministerium of Pennsylvania and Adjacent States and the Muhlenberg Press, 1942–1958.

Parkman, Francis. *The Conspiracy of Pontiac and the Indian*

War After the Conquest of Canada. Boston: Little Brown & Co., 1933.

Post, Christian. "The Journal of Christian Frederick Post." In *Penn Pictures* of *Early Western Pennsylvania,* edited by John Harpster, pp. 68–78. Pittsburgh: University of Pittsburgh Press, 1938.

Richards, Henry Melchior Muhlenberg. "The Pennsylvania German in the French and Indian War." In *The Pennsylvania German Society Proceedings and Addresses* at *Germantown,* Oct. 25, 1904. Vol. XV. Published by the Society, 1906.

Russel, Francis. *The French and Indian Wars.* New York: American Heritage Publishing Co., 1962.

Strassburger, Ralph Beaver, L.L.D., and Hinkle, William John, P.h.D., D.D. "Pennsylvania German Pioneers." In *Pennsylvania German Society Proceedings,* vol. 42, p. 385. Published by the Society, 1934.

Wallace, Paul A. *Indians in Pennsylvania.* Harrisburg: Pennsylvania Historic & Museum Commission, 1970.

————. *Indian Paths of Pennsylvania.* Harrisburg: Pennsylvania Historic & Museum Commission, 1971.